Under Cover
of Night

Books by Jasmine Cresswell

Knave of Hearts
For Love of Christy
One Step to Paradise
Master Touch
Dear Adam
Under Cover of Night
Surprised by Love
Refuge in His Arms
Imprisoned Heart
Tender Triumph
Runaway Love
Stormy Reunion

Under Cover of Night

Jasmine Cresswell

SPEAKING VOLUMES, LLC

NAPLES, FLORIDA

2012

Under Cover of Night

ISBN 978-1-61232-821-8

Chapter One

SOMETIME BETWEEN clearing away the soup bowls and bringing out the baked chicken, Kristin Hamilton decided she was likely to die of boredom before the evening was over. She glanced toward her husband as she carried in the main course, hoping to exchange at least a friendly grimace but, as had happened so often recently, he didn't seem to share her mood. He appeared to be totally absorbed in Professor Aken's lecture.

Lecture was exactly the right word, Kristin thought, placing the platter of chicken in front of Mrs. Aken and trying to smile. The professor always addressed the guests around a dinner table as if they were a gathering of first-year college students who hadn't done their homework. She gritted her teeth and silently offered everybody bacon-stuffed mushrooms. For Grey's sake, she did her best to look interested as she listened to the professor.

1

As far as she could tell, he was discussing an improvement in the catalytic cracking unit of a nearby oil refinery. She wondered idly what a catalytic cracking unit actually was and then decided she didn't care.

"Would you like some sauce for your chicken?" she asked Mrs. Aken when the professor finally paused for a moment. "I should warn you that it has jalapeños in it, so it's rather spicy."

Irene Aken frowned and peered at Kristin over her glasses. "Jalapeños are bad for the digestion," she said. "But the mushrooms look quite good."

"I'm so glad you approve." Kristin opened her green eyes very wide and smiled charmingly. "I would have been devastated if you hadn't liked them."

Fortunately, the Akens were too full of their own importance to know when somebody was putting them on, and Mrs. Aken merely nodded graciously. Kristin glanced at Grey, and this time, to her relief, she saw the answering curve of his mouth and the gleam of appreciation in his dark eyes.

Almost as soon as his gaze met hers, however, his lids drooped, and the hint of a smile disappeared as he turned back to face the professor. "What do you think of Dick Blair's report on coal hydrogenation?" he asked. "Did you happen to read it?"

"Yes, I did. A fascinating article, glad you mentioned it." The professor once again launched into a full-scale dissertation, this time on some project he was supervising for the Colorado School of Mines. Irene Aken and Grey both listened with every appearance of consuming interest.

Seeing that everyone's attention was safely fixed on the professor, Kristin gave up all pretense of concentrating and helped herself to another serving of chicken smothered with spicy sauce. Perhaps the jalapeños would give her violent indigestion. At the moment, even indigestion seemed a less boring prospect than another hour of listening to the professor and her husband swap stories about petroleum sludge.

She spent as long as she could in the kitchen preparing coffee. When she carried in the chocolate cake she had made for dessert, Grey immediately jumped up. She wondered if he was as bored as she was, although there was no way to tell from his manner. She felt a twinge of uneasiness as she realized that, for the past couple of months, she had found it increasingly difficult to judge Grey's mood simply by looking at him. Surely husbands and wives were supposed to find it easier and easier to read each other's feelings, not more and more difficult.

"I'll fetch the coffee, honey," Grey said, going into the kitchen.

"Dessert looks delicious, Kristin," Professor Aken remarked as he accepted a large slice of cake. "Grey claims you're the best cook on campus, and I think he must be right."

"Yes, dinner has been excellent." Mrs. Aken gave Kristin a condescending smile. "It makes a wonderful change to visit you and Grey. Nowadays I find so many young wives have no idea how to serve a decent meal for their families. And as for preparing something special for a dinner party . . . Well, I can't begin to describe some of the horrible meals we've had to sit through!"

"TV dinners still in their foil containers on one occasion," Professor Aken said. "Do you remember, Irene?"

"I certainly do. What's more, my veal patty was frozen in the middle!"

Kristin smiled tightly. "You should have told your hosts to buy a microwave oven. That would have taken care of all their defrosting problems."

Mrs. Aken sniffed. "When I was a young bride, girls took pride in making a real home for their families. In my opinion, there wouldn't be nearly so many broken marriages if today's young women all knew how to cook from scratch and how to iron their husbands' shirts. Not to mention if they knew how to sew on a button."

"What about if the husbands were taught how to cook and how to iron their wives' blouses?" Kristin asked sweetly. "Do you think that would do anything for the divorce rate?"

"Have a cup of coffee, Irene," Grey interjected hastily. "Kristin always adds a touch of almond essence to the beans before she grinds them. It gives the coffee an interesting flavor."

Mrs. Aken accepted a cup of coffee, but she refused to be diverted from her favorite subject. "Most men will never be any good at cooking and sewing," she said, taking Kristin's question entirely at face value. "Even when human beings lived in caves, we women stayed home to care for the little ones while the men went out to hunt for woolly mammoths. You'll find that all this nonsense about working women is just a fad, Kristin. The pendulum swings one way, and then it starts to swing back. Women are soon going to realize that motherhood is the most rewarding career they could ever have."

Kristin tried hard to think of something to say that was both truthful and unprovocative. She was still searching for a reply when Grey's voice broke the silence. She relaxed. Grey was very good at telling little anecdotes that didn't compromise his beliefs yet seemed to support somebody else's opinions.

"You may be right, Irene," he said quietly. "I saw a program on television the other day that said more and more professional women are deciding to start families. Apparently these women once thought their careers would be enough to satisfy them, but now they realize there's something missing from their lives, and they're having children before it's too late. In fact, so many thirty-five-year-olds are having babies that it's producing quite a baby boom."

"Well, I'm not a bit surprised to hear it," Mrs. Aken said smugly. She turned to Kristin. "And how about you, my dear? I hope you're not going to wait until you're a thirty-five-year-old statistic before you have your first child. Grey earns a wonderful salary, and you already have this nice condominium, so there's no reason why you shouldn't start your family right away, is there?"

"No reason at all." Feeling her cheeks flush, she struggled for a measure of self-control. Mrs. Aken had unwittingly touched a very tender nerve. Kristin stood up, avoiding Grey's eyes.

"Would you all excuse me, please? I must have left a pan on the stove. I think I smell something burning."

"Irene? Bill? How about coming into the living room to have a liqueur?" she heard Grey say as she pushed open the kitchen door. "We have Cointreau as well as crème de menthe. And brandy, of course."

Kristin breathed in deeply and kicked the kitchen door hard. It slammed shut with a gratifying bang. She poured hot water over the stack of dirty dishes, deliberately drowning out all sounds of conversation from the other room. She'd be darned if she was coming out of the kitchen until Grey came in to get her, and with any luck that wouldn't be until the Akens were leaving. She'd had a long day at the hospital, and coming home to serve dinner to the Akens definitely amounted to cruel and unusual punishment. Next time Grey wanted to entertain his boss, she thought, he could invite him out to lunch.

It was less than half an hour before the professor and his wife left, both of them warm in their thanks for the wonderful dinner. Kristin closed the front door behind them, then leaned weakly against it.

"Thank heaven they've gone!" she said. "I was afraid I might commit murder before the night was over."

Grey's mouth curved into a grin. "They have hearts of gold, you know, but they were a bit much tonight, weren't they?"

"A bit much!" She stormed into the bedroom, kicking off her shoes and unbuckling her gilt leather belt as she went. Grey followed, picking up her belt and putting her shoes neatly in the walk-in closet.

She went into the bathroom and dashed cold water against her cheeks. "Good lord, Grey, they were more than a bit much! They were intolerable!" She spoke through a mouthful of toothpaste. "Why is it that Mrs. Aken thinks it's all right to make the most offensive statements imaginable, but if we disagreed with her, we'd be told the younger generation has no manners?"

"Hey, calm down, honey. You don't have to see them again for another couple of months, at least, and Irene Aken's views aren't worth getting worked up about."

Kristin was aware of a sudden intense annoyance with her husband. When they had married last year, she had found his calm and his quiet strength a source of comfort, a safe haven after the emotional roller coaster of her childhood. But recently she had begun to feel a little concerned about his perpetually even temper. Her parents fought about everything, yet she knew they loved one another passionately. The gnawing fear, which had begun to occur more and more frequently in recent weeks, clawed once again at her stomach. Perhaps Grey didn't care enough about her to lose his temper.

She paused in the middle of unbuttoning her blouse and began to tug at the combs holding her hair in place. Some demon lurking in a hidden corner of her mind urged her to provoke an argument. Maybe, if she made Grey mad enough, she would break through the strange barrier that seemed to have grown up between them during the past few weeks.

"As far as I can tell, Grey, you don't think anybody's views about anything are worth getting worked up about. I can't remember a single occasion when I've seen you truly angry. Have you ever lost your temper? Do you even know how?"

"Yes," he said, and for a moment it seemed to her that his expression became curiously remote. "Yes, I know how to lose my temper." He bent down to slip off his socks and shoes, then walked into the bathroom. She heard him whistle softly before he began to clean his teeth.

She tossed her hairpins onto the bureau and pulled off her panty hose. "Maybe you agree with Irene Aken," she called out. For some reason, tonight she was spoiling for an argument, and Grey's calm, monosyllabic responses seemed more infuriating by the second. Just for once, dammit, she wanted to know what it would be like to make him mad. Just for once, she wanted to break that infuriating self-control and touch the heart of his passions.

"Maybe you think I should stay home, preparing a tidy little nest for you to come back to every night. Maybe you don't like having a wife who's a physiotherapist."

He came out of the bathroom, his eyes alight with laughter. "And maybe I don't think any of those things. I'm very proud of having a wife who's so good at her job. But I do think I should have been smart enough to steer the conversation away from Irene's pet hobbyhorse. The trouble caused to the world by liberated women is one of her favorite themes. I should have known you'd be foaming at the mouth by the time she left."

His obvious amusement irritated her more than ever, although she had no idea why. "Don't patronize me," she said through clenched teeth.

"I'm not patronizing you. It's just that you have a tendency to get so worked up over ideas and causes that you sometimes forget to look at the real people behind the ideas." He turned away to put his shirt into the laundry hamper, then hung up his slacks neatly on a special hanger and returned them to the closet.

She watched him in silence, all too aware of the sensual magnetism of his lean, tanned body, even when she wanted to be mad at him. She pulled her nightgown over her head with an angry jerk and jumped into bed. "What's that cryptic statement supposed to mean?" she asked.

"It means that sometimes you take people too much at surface value." He picked up her discarded blouse and underclothes, and tucked them tidily into the hamper. "You met Irene Aken nearly a year ago," he said. "Do you know anything at all about her?"

"I know that her views on women and a few dozen other subjects drive me crazy. Isn't that enough?"

Grey sighed. "Probably not. Not if you want to understand the real Irene Aken. She was a mathematician, you know, a very gifted one. When she graduated from Vassar, she was offered the chance to do graduate work at M.I.T. But she gave up all her own career opportunities to marry Bill Aken. In her day it was a rare woman who managed to combine a career with marriage. Society expected women to choose one thing or the other, and Irene chose to marry and become a mother. So you see, it's not surprising that she defends her choice by pretending it was the only rational decision to make."

It was almost impossible to reconcile her impressions of Irene Aken with the information Grey had just given her. Kristin felt a surge of guilt at her misjudgment, accompanied by a strange reluctance to admit just how imperceptive she had been. She turned over, scrunching down under the covers, well away from Grey as he slipped in beside her.

"I suppose the next thing you're going to tell me is that Professor Aken isn't really a pompous old bore but the most brilliant research scientist at the university."

"No. I'm going to tell you that Professor Aken is a pompous old bore *and* the most brilliant research scientist at the university."

There was no mistaking the undercurrent of humor in Grey's voice, and she bit her lip in frustration. She couldn't see him from her position under the blankets, but she could visualize his expression: his hooded lids masking the gleam of lazy laughter in his eyes, the wry quirk to his mouth, the subtle aura of self-control. She realized suddenly that she didn't want Grey to humor her. She wanted . . . she wasn't quite sure what she wanted from him, but she knew it wasn't tolerance or amusement or any of those tame emotions.

She wriggled even farther away from him, confident that he would follow her across the bed. Sure enough, she soon felt his naked body pressing against her back and his fingers tickling her gently at the base of her neck.

"You'd better grab my arm while you have the chance," he said. "There's only about two inches of mattress saving you from a close encounter with the floor."

"Don't tickle me," she murmured weakly, but they both knew her command lacked any semblance of real conviction. She deliberately rolled over onto her stomach to make it more difficult for him to reach her breasts. Part of her wanted to hang on to the remnants of her anger. The other part wanted him to pursue her, to overcome her lingering resistance and make passionate love to her. He curled his arm around her body and stroked her tantalizingly under the chin.

"What are you doing? I'm not a kitten," she mumbled into the pillow.

"I know you're not," he said softly. "You're something much more exciting—a very passionate and desirable woman."

She trembled at his words, feeling desire flood through her. Grey's hands moved down from the hollows of her throat, caressing her breasts through the thin cotton nightgown. She continued lying on her stomach as if she were resisting him, but they both knew she had arched up her rib cage so that his hands would have easier access to her body. They both knew it was only a matter of time until she became a soft, yielding weight in his arms, begging for the ultimate consummation of their lovemaking. He kissed the nape of her neck, teasing her with his tongue, and her body grew hot in pleasurable anticipation.

His fingers skimmed across her long, tangled blond hair, and she felt her pulse begin to throb. He turned her around to face him, kissing her forehead, her eyes, and finally her mouth, while his hands tugged down her nightgown until her breasts were free and he crushed her against him. He parted her lips with his tongue, murmuring words of desire against her mouth.

"Oh God, Kris, you're so beautiful. I could die from wanting you."

She murmured something in reply, she wasn't sure what because she could rarely think coherently once Grey began to make love to her. His hands gradually crept over her stomach to her thighs, and his mouth turned her skin to fire so that her mind was consumed by the powerful sensations he created in her body.

It was always like this when they made love. In bed, in the heated darkness of the night, Grey seemed to become a different person, as if he were accustomed to taking command and expecting instant response to his orders. And yet, despite the dominating role he took in their sexual relationship, he showed such sensitivity to her needs and feelings that she felt closer to Grey when they made love than she did at any other time.

He kissed her throat and her breasts as his hands continued to weave their magic patterns. She clasped her hands around his neck and molded the curves of her body into the hollows of his. He caressed her spine with languorous, tickling strokes, then held her slightly away, moving down in the bed so that he could nuzzle her stomach with slow, circular movements of his mouth. She had a sudden erotic image of what it would be like to be pregnant with his child, and her womb seemed to contract in a sharp ache of longing.

"I want to have your baby, Grey," she whispered impulsively, too entranced by his lovemaking to consider her words. "Mrs. Aken was right about one thing: There's no reason for us to wait any longer to have a child."

She felt the immediate stiffening of his body and wished fervently that she had never spoken. She hadn't meant to reintroduce the old argument. It had become a threatening subject over the past few weeks, almost the only topic that seemed able to disturb the iron-hard surface of Grey's self-control. Lying in his arms like this, she could sense his emotional withdrawal. She could almost feel the way he closed in upon himself, drawing his thoughts inward, out of her reach, even though he continued to cradle her in his arms.

She held her breath, but it was only a second or so before he spoke, and, when he did, his voice remained light and affectionate. If they hadn't been wrapped in each other's arms, she never would have guessed that his feelings were so deeply touched. He was, she realized with a sense of shock, very good at pretending.

"There's at least one excellent reason to wait," he said. "And I'm the reason. I don't want to have a baby right now, Kris. Believe me, it's not the right time for us to start a family."

"But I'm twenty-seven, and you're thirty-four. If I wait until I'm in my thirties to have a baby, you'll be nearly forty before our child celebrates its first birthday."

"Good lord, to think senility is so close at hand and I'd never noticed! Remind me tomorrow to make inquiries about hair transplants before it's too late." He raised himself on one elbow, staring down at her as he touched the soft curve of her cheek. "Honey, it's six years until I'm forty. We could have produced quadruplets by then."

He began to stroke her stomach again, and she put her hand over his, holding it tightly, as if the physical contact of their fingers could help her understand why he always placed the idea of having a child so firmly in the future. It hadn't been this way to begin with. Last year, when they were first married, he had often said how much he looked forward to seeing her pregnant with his baby. She had been the one who suggested they wait a few months. How bitterly she now regretted that decision!

She turned her face into the pillow, muffling her words in its soft feathers, reluctant to pursue the subject and yet somehow unable to leave it alone. "Please, Grey, it's not enough just to say you don't want to have a baby right now. Can't you explain why you don't want me to get pregnant?" She forced herself to express her deepest fear. "Don't you think I'd make a good mother for your child?"

"I think you'd make an excellent mother," he said quietly. "Hey, Kris, don't go reading hidden meanings into everything I say. I love you. One day I want you to be the mother of my children. Can't you just accept that I'm not ready to be a father right at this particular moment?"

"I suppose I'll have to. I don't seem to have any other choice."

"Face it, honey, limited options are part of the human condition. As far as I know, there's nobody around to guarantee that life will always be fair in dealing out chances."

She was startled by the unusual harshness in his voice. Grey had never been in the habit of making cynical reflections on the meaning of life, and she didn't know how to react to this one. She felt a brief moment of panic. This cynicism was just one more example of the subtle changes she had noticed in her husband recently, and she was worried by all of them. Grey was her rock, her oasis of calm after the stormy seas of her childhood. She had spent her teenage years struggling to cope with her parents' monumental egos and volatile artistic temperaments. One of the reasons she had been attracted to Grey was that he seemed to represent everything that was solid and normal, everything that was organized and controlled. She wasn't ready to discover too many hidden depths in her relationship with him.

The last trace of desire trickled away from her, squeezed out by the confusion of her emotions. She didn't want to continue the discussion; she was afraid suddenly that it might turn into a real argument. She eased herself out of his arms, giving them both an excuse to avoid any further confrontation. She glanced at the lighted dial of the alarm clock.

"Heavens, look at the time! I had no idea it was so late." Her voice was high with false brightness. "It's past midnight, and my first patient is scheduled for seven-thirty. We'd better get some sleep."

"Sleep isn't exactly uppermost in my mind right now," Grey murmured, and even in the darkness of the bedroom she could see the gleam of his smile. Before she could say anything further, his hand brushed swiftly down her stomach and nestled between her thighs. She shivered with instinctive pleasure as his fingers began to tease her into renewed passion, and it was only a few moments before her cheeks were flushed with the heat of reawakened desire.

His body was hard against her thigh; his breath was warm in her ear.

"Are you sure you want to go to sleep?" he asked softly. His voice soothed her troubled feelings with its tender hint of laughter. "I don't want to disturb you if you're feeling tired."

"I'm not tired anymore." She shuddered within the strong circle of his arms. Her mouth opened against his, and she murmured his name in a hoarse plea for fulfillment. He looked at her intently, searching her face as she trembled on the verge of ecstasy, then he put his hands beneath her hips and arched her body away from the bed. All hint of laughter vanished from his dark eyes as he lifted her body to accept the thrust of his possession.

She had time only for a single glimpse of his face—strong, fierce, and elemental in its passion—before the world fell away in a swift explosion of hot, shivering blackness.

I love you. She thought he gasped out the words against the tangled mass of her hair. But afterward, when Grey was asleep and her body and mind were functioning normally once again, she couldn't be certain he had spoken the words. Maybe she had only heard the echo of her own frantic cry.

Chapter Two

KRISTIN HAD A busy schedule at the hospital the next day, but, for once, her mind was not fully on her work. She helped an elderly, bedridden man exercise in the warm whirlpool; she massaged the shrunken limbs of a middle-aged woman who had been a childhood victim of polio; she guided the first postoperative steps of a toddler who had recently undergone reconstructive surgery; and she dealt with a whole crop of torn ligaments and wrenched muscles suffered during a community college football game.

Beneath the reassuring cheerfulness of her smiles, however, Kristin's thoughts tumbled in confusion. She had felt a growing uneasiness about her marriage over the past few weeks, and last night the uneasiness had finally crystallized into something more threatening. She acknowledged to herself that she had never been entirely

sure of Grey's feelings for her, even though his personality seemed so open and easygoing. She realized now,
as she hadn't when they'd first met, that Grey's lighthearted banter formed a highly effective barricade that
protected his deepest feelings. She had never quite known
how to reach him, never known how to touch the heart
of his emotions, and recently it seemed that the gap
between their surface relationship and their true feelings
was growing wider. At least in bed, even if nowhere
else, she had once thought that their harmony was perfect. But during the past couple of weeks even that method
of communication seemed to have become fraught with
a curious new tension.

Kristin concentrated on massaging Mrs. Berry's wasted
limbs with firm, careful movements, trying to avoid giving unnecessary pain as she exercised the paralyzed muscles. But however hard she concentrated on her
professional chores, the nagging fear at the back of her
mind wouldn't go away. The more time she spent in
Grey's company, the more she learned to love him. What
if his feelings for her had followed the opposite path?
What if he no longer loved her? That would certainly
explain why he didn't want her to have his baby. Maybe
he thought their marriage was a mistake. Maybe he wanted
to end it, but was simply too kindhearted to tell her the
truth.

The mere thought of ending her marriage to Grey was
enough to make her stomach lurch in panic, but she
forced herself to examine the possibility. Grey knew how
much she treasured security and stability; perhaps he was
trying to find some way to break the news to her gently.
He was the only person who knew the truth about her
unusual childhood. He knew how she had spent most of
her youth trailing around the world in the wake of her
parents. Growing up as the only child of a world-famous
conductor and an equally famous opera singer would
probably be difficult for any child, but since she was

tone-deaf, Kristin's problems had been increased a hundred times over.

It was Grey who had taught her to see the humorous side of her family situation. It was Grey who had encouraged her to laugh at the memory of her disastrous early music lessons. He had actually made her giggle over the stories about her bewildered parents trying to decide where their tone-deaf daughter had sprung from. It was Grey who finally convinced her that the entire world did not revolve around opera houses and concert platforms—that millions of people had never heard an opera or a symphony and, what's more, had no desire to hear one.

She would always be grateful to Grey for the support he had given her, for the way he had encouraged her to take pride in her own achievements as a physiotherapist. Looking back over the months of their marriage, however, Kristin couldn't think of any comparable gift she had given her husband. He had always seemed so incredibly competent and so totally self-sufficient.

She narrowed her thoughts to the last two months. She remembered all the strange, tight little moments of silence. She remembered the numerous phone calls that turned out to be wrong numbers. She thought about the sudden inexplicable increase in Grey's travel schedule. She remembered all the late nights he had spent at the university "catching up on paperwork." She remembered it all, and her heart sank to the soles of her sensible white shoes.

Traffic was still heavy even though it was late when she left the hospital and drove along I-25 toward home. She switched on the radio, listening to the news and the sunny forecast for Denver tomorrow with less than half her attention. Her thoughts drifted back to the subject of her marriage, and Kristin gave herself a brisk mental talking-to. She was becoming paranoid, she decided. She had no reason to suspect that there was some vital aspect of her husband's life she didn't understand, some important facet of his personality that he kept deliberately hidden. The first year of married life was notoriously bumpy. It was time for her to be thankful for all the good times she shared with Grey and to put her stupid suspicions aside.

Grey was already home when she let herself into the apartment. He greeted her with a warm smile and a long, satisfying kiss, his hands cupping her breasts with casual, comforting possessiveness. She returned his embrace eagerly, her worries of the afternoon fading into a distant corner of her mind.

"I was going to cook dinner for us," he said, keeping her in his arms. "Then I had a better idea and called a restaurant for reservations. We're supposed to be there at eight o'clock, so you'd better change fast."

"That was a great idea!" She hurried into the bedroom, tugging at the belt of her uniform. "Did you choose somewhere nice?"

"The best. Don Pasquale's." He followed her into their room, sitting on the bed while she rummaged in the closet for a suitable dress. "I missed you this evening," he said. "What held you up? Problems with one of your patients?"

"Sort of. I got delayed working with Tom Mareno. You remember him, the teenager from Englewood I told you about?"

"The one who'd been partying and had an accident with his motorcycle?"

"Yes." She pulled all the pins out of her hair and brushed it fiercely. "Tom's just realized that he's probably never going to walk again without crutches, and he's in a state of shock. He was one of the high school's superjocks, captain of the basketball team, all that kind of stuff, and he isn't interested in learning how to keep his body fit now that he can't ski down a mountain or lead the school's winning team. His legs aren't paralyzed, but as far as he's concerned, they might as well be. He doesn't want to hear about exercises to stop the muscles from atrophying. He doesn't want to hear about occupational therapy or retraining. We had a very frustrating session. I was angry with him, and he's mad at the whole world."

Grey held out her jacket, and she slipped her arms into it. "Tom'll come around," he said. "You know you're great at persuading kids to make the best of whatever physical abilities they have."

She sighed. "I'll tell you, working with Tom this evening, I didn't seem to be too great at persuading anybody to do anything."

Grey locked the front door, and they walked together to the elevator. "I suppose victims of traffic accidents must be some of the most difficult patients to treat."

"Yes, they are. I just wish kids like Tom wouldn't think they have to drink a six-pack of beer and then drive too fast in order to prove they're men. Some days I can't bear having to work with the results of their fantasies. It seems such a waste."

"But other days there are compensations." Grey grinned at her, deliberately trying to lighten her mood. "Think of that wonderful afternoon when you walked into your office and found me lying on the examining table. All six handsome feet of me. All naked and all yours."

She smiled, responding to his teasing. "One masculine body draped in a sheet looks very much like another," she said primly.

"I seem to remember you got rid of the sheet pretty darn fast."

"I was assessing the extent of your injuries," she said with dignity.

"Oh yes, I'm sure you were. I could tell all those tender strokes along my spine were strictly for professional assessment!"

They stepped out of the elevator into the underground parking garage, and Kristin did her best to remain on her dignity. "For your information, Mr. Grey Hamilton, you didn't even have an interesting medical problem."

"It felt interesting to me, let me tell you!"

"Torn cartilage can be painful," she agreed, getting into their car. "And you were very badly bruised. Your body looked like you'd fallen off a mountain."

There was a tiny pause. "Not quite," he said.

"You know, I treated a parachutist once whose chute hadn't opened properly, and he had injuries that were pretty much like yours." She stared at Grey with a sudden surge of curiosity. "I never could understand how you got so many bruises just from tumbling downstairs. You looked as if you'd fallen incredibly hard, and from a considerable height."

He sighed in mock dismay. "Honey, I did fall from a great height. It's a long way from the top to the bottom of a flight of stairs, particularly when you bump each stair as you go down."

"You're not usually so clumsy," she said, and realized as she spoke that he was, in fact, one of the most agile men she had ever met. She looked at him, aware of yet another fact that had puzzled her subconsciously for a long time. "Do you know, Grey, for a guy who doesn't play any sports, you're amazingly fit."

"I do work out at the university gym occasionally," he said. "In fact, I work out most days."

"Yes, I guess that would keep you fit." She dismissed the puzzle from her mind, and they drove into the restaurant parking lot, talking about nothing in particular as they strolled into the lobby and waited to check their jackets. Although the temperature had reached the high seventies that day, the night air in Denver was always chilly.

Two men, neither of them drunk but both decidedly merry, were collecting their coats from the cloakroom. One of the men disappeared in the direction of the rest room, and the other continued his noisy flirtation with the girl behind the counter. Kristin, thinking of Tom Mareno and all her other drunk-driving patients, hoped the men were going to take a taxi home.

The man finally gave up his flirtation and turned around to beam in a friendly, unfocused fashion at everybody within view. His bleary gaze wandered past Kristin and fixed itself on Grey. His face immediately lit up with surprise and pleasure.

"Why, Paul, you old son-of-a-gun!" he exclaimed. He thumped Grey vigorously on the shoulder, grabbing his hand and pumping it up and down. "Fancy seeing you here! I thought you were supposed to be holding down the fort in Washington."

Grey smiled easily. "Sorry to disappoint you, sir, but I'm afraid you've made a mistake. I'm not Paul."

The man frowned, too close to drunkenness to be tactful. "What the hell! Of course you're Paul. You're Paul Mason. Dammit, Paul, we had lunch together half a dozen times last year! We talked about the new technology for—" Some warning bell seemed to penetrate the haze of alcohol fogging the man's brain. "Anyway, we had lunch. You know me, Paul, you old devil. I'm Harry Gilmore."

Grey's smile didn't waver. Kristin thought that only somebody who knew him very well would have sensed the extraordinary tension coiling within him. "Maybe I have a double, Mr. Gilmore, but I'm definitely not the man you think I am. If you'll excuse me?"

"He's not Paul Mason," Kristin interjected, trying to be helpful. "This is my husband. His name's Gre—"

Grey tugged so hard on her arm that she stopped in mid-word. "What's the matter?" she asked him, almost forgetting Harry Gilmore in her astonishment.

"The maître d' is waiting to take us to our table," Grey said. "Come on, honey. I'm starving, even if you're not." He propelled Kristin firmly in the direction of the main dining room, leaving Harry Gilmore standing in the lobby. Kristin glanced behind her and saw that he was staring after them, his mouth hanging slightly open as he tried to collect his alcohol-clouded wits.

She was surprised by the urgency with which Grey had pushed her toward their table. "What was that all about?" she asked. She gave him a teasing smile, although something about the incident had made her very uncomfortable. "Are you leading a secret life, Grey? Do you go into telephone booths, spin around twice, and emerge as Paul Mason, secret associate of Mr. Harry Gilmore?"

"Nope. Sorry to be so boring, but I only go into phone booths when I have to make a phone call. And if I went into a telephone booth right now, however many times I spun around, I'd come out as plain old Grey Hamilton. A starving Grey Hamilton, in fact. I missed lunch today."

"So did I." She forced herself to relax. "I'm glad you decided to make reservations here tonight. I wasn't in the mood to cook."

For a few minutes their attention was absorbed by the menu, but when they had given their selections to the waiter, Kristin found her thoughts returning to the strange incident with Harry Gilmore.

"That man was so sure he knew you," she said. "Who do you think he confused you with? Maybe Paul Mason really is your double."

"Kris, Mr. Gilmore had obviously consumed enough alcohol to pickle his brains. It isn't so surprising that he thought I was his long-lost buddy. The only really surprising thing is that he didn't think you were his favorite girl friend—or maybe his mother!"

She laughed. "The poor guy wasn't that drunk, Grey."

"He was drunk enough to be a nuisance."

The waiter arrived at that moment with their meals, and they sat quietly while he placed the steaming platters of paella in front of them.

"Mmm . . . this is so good," Kristin said, taking a large bite of rice and shrimp. "I like Spanish food in Denver so much better than I liked Spanish food in Spain."

"Are you sure you've got that the right way around?" Grey sounded amused.

"Oh, yes. I spent two or three months in Madrid when I was about sixteen. My mother was singing in operas all over Spain, and my father was commuting to Paris to conduct the symphony there. We took a hotel suite near the airport so that we'd have some sort of base for the summer. I discovered that Spanish chefs pride themselves on their garnishes. I'd order something simple like grilled fish, and the waiter would bring it with a side order of boiled baby eels. And then my parents' Spanish friends were always encouraging me to try their favorite dishes. I decided that summer that musicians must have some sort of weird fetish for octopus. I can't tell you how many times people made me eat octopus."

Grey's smile was sympathetic. "I gather it doesn't taste too good?"

"It tastes like fried rubber bands."

"Have another glass of wine," Grey said. Their eyes met over the rims of their glasses, and they both burst out laughing.

It was a wonderful meal. While they studied the dessert menu, Kristin kicked off her shoes and ran her stockinged feet seductively up and down the insides of Grey's legs. With secret delight she watched the flush darkening across his cheekbones.

Finally he uttered a small groan. "You have to stop that," he said.

She ran her toes right up to his groin, resting one foot in his lap and allowing the other to wander. "Stop what?" she asked, her green eyes wide and full of false innocence.

"Oh, nothing, I guess." His own gaze suddenly became as innocent as her own. Under cover of the long tablecloth, his hand slid along her leg and pushed up the soft folds of her dress. His fingers traced a delicate pattern, traveling inexorably above her knee.

"Don't, Grey!" she gasped. "You can't! Not here!"

The waiter arrived to take their orders for dessert. Grey politely handed him back the menus. "I don't believe we'll have dessert after all. My wife is in a hurry to get home." His smile was a miracle of blandness as he turned toward Kristin. "Isn't that right, darling?"

"Er—yes." She was sure she had blushed bright scarlet from her neck to the roots of her hair, and she hardly waited for the waiter to turn away before stuffing her feet into her shoes.

"Grey, how could you!" she exclaimed.

"Easily. And I notice you still haven't asked me to take my hand away."

Kristin rested her head on Grey's shoulder during the short drive home. As soon as they entered the apartment, he took her into his arms, kissing her deeply and wrapping his arms around her underneath her jacket. She snuggled up to him, resting her head comfortably against his chest. It felt absolutely right to be held in his arms.

"What shall we do this weekend?" she asked when Grey finally moved away from her to lock and bolt the front door. "How about driving into the foothills to see if the aspen leaves have started to turn color?"

"Sounds like a good idea, but—" The sharp ring of the telephone interrupted their conversation, and Kristin stepped into the kitchen to answer it.

"Grey Hamilton, please," said a crisp, masculine voice. The caller didn't identify himself.

"It's for you," she said, holding out the instrument to Grey. "Sounds like long-distance."

Grey took the phone. "Hello?"

He was silent for a considerable time. "I'll handle it," she heard Grey say as she walked into the bedroom. She heard nothing more of the conversation, although the apartment walls were thin and the kitchen was next to the bedroom. Either Grey wasn't saying much, or he was keeping his voice extraordinarily low.

At last he entered the bedroom, tugging at his tie. "That was an old college friend. He wants me to head up this year's alumni appeal."

"Oh," Kristin said. "What's his name?"

"His name?" There was an infinitesimal pause. "Sam," Grey said. "His name's Sam Meyer."

Kristin made no comment, chiefly because she wasn't quite sure how you set about accusing your husband of lying. She slid under the covers, watching Grey as he undressed. Her pulse began to race with undeniable sexual attraction, and she wondered how one instinct could tell you that your husband was lying at the same time that another instinct urged you to make passionate, abandoned love with him.

"So what about this weekend?" she asked finally. "Shall we drive into the foothills? The weather forecast's good."

Grey seemed unnecessarily preoccupied with the contents of the bedroom closet. "I'm sorry, Kris," he said, not turning around. "I should have told you earlier, but this weekend I'm going to be away. It's another business meeting, I'm afraid. I have to go to Buffalo."

She inhaled sharply. "Buffalo! You never mentioned anything about going to Buffalo! Why do you need to go there?" Hearing how shrill her questions sounded, she forced herself to calm down. "Why would anybody have to go to Buffalo?" she asked, relieved to note that her voice sounded considerably quieter.

Grey emerged from the closet, his grin rueful. "You make it sound like the end of the universe. There are some good reasons to go there, you know. It's right by Niagara Falls, after all, and just across the border from Canada. The mayor of Buffalo has a whole new promotion scheme going. He's trying to persuade the American people that Buffalo is the up-and-coming vacation center of the Northeast."

"There has to be another reason you're going there. The mayor can't be that convincing, no matter what advertising agency he's hired."

"The National Association of Geologists is holding its annual conference at the Buffalo Convention Center this weekend. Professor Aken is presenting a paper on the work we're doing, and naturally I have to go."

"I see. I wish you'd mentioned it earlier." She looked away as he got into bed beside her. "You've been traveling an awful lot recently, Grey."

"Yes, I have. This seems to be a busy time for me. I'm sorry. I hate leaving you alone over the weekend, but I have to catch a five o'clock plane tomorrow evening. I'm afraid we can't even have dinner together before I leave."

"Never mind."

The strange tension that had so often afflicted them in recent weeks once again stretched tightly between them. Kristin felt choked by its presence, yet she didn't want to examine its cause too closely. She was afraid of what she might discover if she probed too deeply. She lay down, resting her head on her hands in a fair imitation of casualness.

"I'll call one of my friends at the hospital," she said. "We can go out for a pizza, then take in a movie or something."

"I'll miss you," Grey said huskily. "I'll be thinking of you all weekend."

"Will you?" The question burst out before she could stop it.

"Hey, Kris, what do you mean? Of course I'll be thinking of you."

He took her hand and stroked it slowly across his tanned chest and down over his stomach. "I'll be thinking of you doing this to me," he murmured. He leaned over and ran his tongue tantalizingly across her lower lip. "And I'll be thinking of doing this," he said. "And this," he murmured as he kissed her. "And this," he said, sliding down her body to caress her breasts.

She gave a tiny, involuntary groan of pleasure, twisting her body to fit more tightly against his. "And I'll definitely be imagining you moaning like that," he whispered.

"I wasn't moaning," she protested.

She saw the laughter gleam in his eyes just before he flicked off the light. "Well, sweetheart, I'm sorry to hear that, but I promise I'll have you moaning soon."

In the early hours of the morning, Kristin got up to get a drink of water. She switched on the bathroom light, then stood for a moment in the doorway, looking at her husband. He was lying on his stomach, deeply asleep, his head partially buried in the pillow. His shoulders were uncovered, and she felt a sharp clench of erotic sensation as she saw how the pale blue sheets emphasized his dark tan and the supple strength of his muscles. Even in sleep he displayed none of the vulnerability she would have expected. The lines of his body still seemed to carry a hint of tension, a suggestion that he would wake at the slightest unusual sound to instant alertness.

Grey turned in his sleep, and Kristin smiled at her own vivid imagination. As she returned to her side of the bed, the idea of joining Grey in Buffalo suddenly sprang full-blown into her mind. It might not be exactly the ideal city for a romantic weekend, but perhaps they could cross the border into Canada and have dinner at a restaurant overlooking Niagara. She had never seen the falls, and they were considered one of the natural wonders of the world. Perhaps away from home and in unfamiliar surroundings she would be able to pinpoint precisely what was troubling her about their marriage. At least she might find the right words to explain to Grey how so many little incidents over the past few weeks had contributed to her feeling of anxiety.

For some reason the encounter with Harry Gilmore in the restaurant sprang into her mind. The man had been so certain he knew her husband, so certain that Grey was Paul Mason.

Kristin gave an impatient shrug, faintly annoyed by her irrational train of thought. She smoothed the sheet around her shoulders and began to make practical plans for the trip. Tomorrow, fortunately, she was already scheduled to leave the hospital at four. She would beg a favor from one of her colleagues and have somebody take over her last couple of patients. That way she would be able to leave work a couple of hours early. She would have time to throw a few clothes into a suitcase and hop a cab to the airport. Grey would be so surprised to see her at the check-in line!

She thought about the new black lace nightgown she had never worn. She would definitely take that with her. She had a new peacock-green suit, too, which did spectacular things to her eyes.

Kristin was smiling when she fell asleep.

Chapter Three

As if to compensate for the frustration of the previous few weeks, Friday was a great day at the hospital for Kristin. Three of her routine postoperative patients were well enough to return home. Missy Gordon, the five-year-old victim of a hit-and-run driver, took several tottering but unaided steps across the treatment room. Only two months earlier surgeons had feared she might never get out of her wheelchair. Tom Mareno, the Englewood high school student, shuffled shamefacedly into Kristin's office on his crutches and said he guessed maybe he would like to enroll in a physical rehabilitation program. And Grey telephoned at lunchtime to tell Kristin how much he was going to miss her over the weekend.

"Don't worry about it," she said, smiling with secret delight. He sounded so lonely that she almost revealed her plans to join him, but in the end she decided it would be more fun to keep her arrival a surprise.

"I'm sure I'll find something to do to keep me out of mischief," she added teasingly.

"I have all sorts of useful suggestions," Grey said. "The guest bathroom needs painting, for one."

She laughed. Redecorating the second bathroom had been on their list of urgent projects for at least four months.

"No way, friend," she said. "If I'd wanted to be my own house painter, I wouldn't have gotten married! As far as I'm concerned, painting and decorating are definitely a husband's lot in life."

"How come when my shirts need ironing you're an independent, liberated woman, but when the bathroom ceiling needs attention, you're suddenly a helpless, old-fashioned female?"

"It's just another one of life's little mysteries, I guess. I'll be happy to discuss all aspects of the problem with you next time you're home."

"I can think of more interesting ways to spend our time," he said huskily.

Her breath caught on a tiny sigh of pleasurable anticipation. "I'll be happy to discuss those with you, too," she murmured.

Even over the phone she was aware of a sudden change in Grey's manner. "Hey, honey, I have to go. Somebody's waiting to brief—to speak to me. See you on Sunday night. I love you. Bye."

"I love you, too." Kristin spoke to the purr of an empty line, but she hung up the phone in a mood close to euphoria. She had a feeling deep in her bones that this weekend was going to be something really special.

She called out a round of thanks to her colleagues as she left the hospital, then drove home admiring the cloudless blue sky and the sharp, sunlit silhouette of the Rocky Mountains to the west. She was lucky that Grey's work enabled them to live in such an attractive city as Denver. She was lucky, too, that her own professional qualifications were so much in demand that she could move almost anywhere in the States and still expect to find employment.

She had time for a relaxing bath when she arrived back at the apartment. Wrapped in a large towel, she spent a delightful twenty minutes rummaging through her drawers and closet, looking for the sexiest clothes she could find to pack in her weekend suitcase.

Her blond hair was thick and naturally wavy and miraculously easy to care for. She brushed it vigorously, then swept it up into a loose chignon that somehow managed to look neat and seductive at the same time. She put on her new peacock-green suit and a pale silk blouse, touching color to her lips and cheeks but not bothering with any other makeup.

When she looked in the mirror, she felt a fresh surge of elation. Her new outfit highlighted the emerald flecks in her hazel eyes and flattered the creamy pallor of her complexion. She knew she looked her best, and she was suddenly quite sure that she had made the right decision about the upcoming weekend. It was exactly what she and Grey needed to get their relationship back on track again.

It was a good thing she wasn't superstitious, Kristin decided, when she arrived at Stapleton Airport and found a parking place almost at the door opposite the airline counter. Everything today was going so incredibly smoothly that a pessimist would have wondered what horror was lurking just around the corner. She hadn't even encountered any traffic snarl-ups, so she was a little earlier than she needed to be. So much the better, she thought. She was almost certain to spot Grey as soon as he arrived.

She grabbed her purse and suitcase, locked the car doors, and hummed tunelessly but contentedly as she walked toward the terminal building. If only her poor mother could hear her now, she thought, and suppressed a sudden urge to giggle. Not only off-key, but humming a song from the current top ten hits. As a child she had been brought up to believe that the arias from *La Bohème* or *Aïda* constituted the ultimate in light entertainment. She had spent so much of her youth with dedicated professional musicians that it had been a revelation to discover as a teenager that most young people didn't relax by listening to eighteenth-century baroque chamber music. It had been an even greater revelation to meet Grey and discover, with his encouragement, that once she stopped worrying about her own lack of talent, she could actually enjoy listening to classical music.

The travel agent had arranged for her to pick up her ticket at the airline counter. She kept an eye open for Grey as she stood in line at the check-in desk, but he was nowhere in sight. He disliked hanging around at airports waiting for flights to depart, so she wasn't surprised by his absence.

"I have a reservation on your four forty-five flight to Buffalo," she said to the clerk when it was finally her turn to check in. "I'm Kristin Hamilton. Do you have my ticket? The travel agent said it would be here."

"Oh, yes, Mrs. Hamilton. I have it right in this drawer." The reservations clerk produced the ticket with a smile. Kristin planned to carry her small suitcase onto the plane, so the clerk directed her immediately toward the security screening area.

"The Buffalo flight leaves from Concourse B, Gate 12," she said. "The flight will be boarding shortly, so you should go through right away."

Kristin thanked her and walked off toward the security area, stopping on the way to examine an enticing display of paperbacks. The flight was going to take nearly four hours, so it would be a good time to catch up on some reading. It was ages since she'd curled up to enjoy a lighthearted best-seller.

She had no idea what made her glance up from her examination of two books whose covers promised "swashbuckling adventure and heart-stopping romance on every page." One moment she was trying to decide whether to cast her lot with pirates in the Caribbean or a decadent duke in Tuscany, the next her gaze was drawn irresistibly toward the throng of people clustered at the entrance to the security screening section of the airport.

She spotted Grey's thick, black hair right away and wondered with a touch of amusement whether his marital radar system was working as efficiently as hers. Although she could see only his shoulders and the back of his head above the crowd, she had recognized him immediately. He didn't seem to be walking in the direction of the Buffalo check-in line.

She hastily pushed the two fat books back into the rack and raised her hand in an enthusiastic greeting.

He didn't see her wave, but she hurried eagerly toward him, dodging around travelers who all seemed to be moving in the opposite direction. Despite the mill of bodies, she was gradually catching up with Grey and would soon be close enough to say his name without needing to yell. She paused to catch her breath to call out, and at that precise moment the crowd surrounding him finally parted.

He wasn't alone. A young woman, so petite she had been entirely hidden from Kristin's view, clung possessively to his arm.

Kristin stood immobile in the middle of the concourse. After a while she realized that her mouth was still open ready to call Grey's name. With a distinct effort of will, she snapped her jaws shut. A man bumped into her and muttered a hurried apology. A little boy brushed his sticky lollipop against the skirt of her new suit; she scarcely heard his mother's embarrassed excuses.

At last some primitive instinct, akin to the one that sends a wounded animal scurrying for cover, forced her body into motion. She slipped behind a convenient pillar, her heart pounding as if *she* were guilty of some terrible misdemeanor and afraid of being discovered. She breathed a shaky sigh of relief when Grey and the woman moved through the security checkpoint and out of her sight.

As soon as they were gone, a different sort of panic seized her. She had scarcely glanced at the woman, didn't even remember what she looked like. All she had seen was the woman's hand, slender, pink-tipped, and elegant — and stretched possessively along Grey's forearm. She had to know what this woman was like, this woman who was going away with Grey for the weekend.

She started forward, her body seeming to move without instructions from her brain, and then common sense suddenly returned. What was happening to her? Had she gone crazy? Why was she assuming Grey and this woman were spending the weekend together? She had seen her husband and a young woman enter the airport arm in arm. There were probably a dozen logical explanations as to what they were doing here, other than that they were planning to spend an illicit weekend with each other. Relief washed over her in an overwhelming wave.

She placed her purse and suitcase on the security scanning belt and walked through the metal-detector arch. By the time she retrieved her belongings from the X-ray machine, she was perfectly calm again. For some reason not quite clear to her, however, she didn't walk openly along the wide hallway. She sought the protection of little clusters of passersby, walking always in the middle of a group as her gaze searched restlessly for Grey and his companion.

She found them at the departure gate for a five-ten flight leaving for Washington, D.C. She watched with a curiously detached interest as Grey escorted the woman to one of the huge viewing windows and they leaned against it, their flight bags stacked at their feet.

The woman wasn't quite as young as Kristin had imagined in that first, shocked glimpse. She was at least thirty, possibly more, with a delicate, graceful body and a fragile, faintly exotic face. Kristin had a fleeting impression that she had seen the woman somewhere before, but she realized her impressions at this moment were too confused to be reliable. The woman's hair was raven dark, swept into a low, classic chignon at the nape of her neck, where it gleamed with a lustrous, blue-black sheen. She was almost as dark as Grey, Kristin thought. A perfect match for him.

She bit back a sudden sob of painful laughter, forcing herself to watch impassively as Grey lowered his head to hear whatever the woman was saying. He put his arm around her shoulders, then reached out to touch her cheek with a gentleness that struck Kristin like a harsh blow. For some reason she had the impression he was wiping away a tear from his companion's face. In return, the woman nestled her cheek lovingly against the back of his hand. To Kristin, the gesture seemed more intimate than a kiss.

"Are you all right, miss? Miss? Would you like me to get you a drink of water? You look like you're gonna pass out."

Kristin blinked. "Oh, I'm sorry. I didn't realize you were talking to me." She drew in a gulp of air. "I'm fine, thanks. Just fine."

"Seen somebody off on a plane, have you?" The elderly man was determined to be sympathetic. "That's always depressing. I'm a widower, and my daughter lives in Philadelphia. That's why I'm here. I came to see her off. She's a long way away, sure enough, but with all these new jet planes you can soon catch up with somebody, can't you? It's not like when I was a young man."

"No, it certainly isn't." Kristin scarcely recognized her own voice, it sounded so cold. "I'm sure you're right. There's nothing like a modern airport for helping you catch up with somebody."

The elderly man made another encouraging remark — she didn't hear what. The imminent departure of Flight 271 for Washington, D.C., was announced over the public-address system. Grey and the woman—the Other Woman, Kristin thought with a silent tremor of hysterical laughter—walked toward the boarding tunnel. His arm held her protectively within its circle. Her head rested trustingly against his shoulder. At that precise moment Kristin hated them both.

She had absolutely no recollection of getting into her car and driving back to the apartment. She turned out the contents of her purse and discovered she must have returned to the airline counter and claimed a refund on her unused ticket to Buffalo. She was amazed by the efficiency of her subconscious mind. She stared for a long time at the refund slip, wondering how on earth she could have conducted an entire conversation that was now wiped completely from her mind.

She hung her clothes in the closet with great neatness, carefully removing the lollipop stain from her suit skirt before draping the outfit on its special satin hanger. When all her clothes were in immaculate order and her suitcase was stowed once again on its high shelf, she glanced at her watch. It was only seven o'clock. An eternity seemed to have passed since she set off from the apartment four hours earlier, but there were still three hours left before she could even consider going to bed. What was she going to do for three whole hours?

Panic engulfed her then, the black, gut-wrenching realization that she couldn't just ignore what she had seen at the airport. She couldn't pretend she had never been there, never seen Grey with another woman. The brutal fact was that her husband had lied to her, and probably more than once. It would be foolish to deny the evidence of her own eyes. She had seen him board a plane destined for Washington with a stunningly attractive woman hanging onto his arm. She had to face up to the implications of what she had seen.

But not right now. Not for another minute or so. Maybe she was still leaping to false conclusions. Kristin walked over to the bookshelf and pulled down an atlas. Geography had never been her strong point. Perhaps Washington was on the way to Buffalo. After all, Grey had never said precisely which flight he was taking. She had simply assumed he would fly direct.

She stared for a long time at the map before closing the atlas and returning it tidily to its place on the shelf. She had run out of excuses. Nobody would choose to fly from Denver to Buffalo via Washington, not when there was a direct flight leaving at almost the same time.

She went into the kitchen and made herself a pot of tea. It was a relief to have something to do with her hands since the practical task seemed to stop them from shaking. She waited for the kettle to boil, acknowledging the bitter truth that she had never really believed her marriage to Grey would last. She had always nurtured a secret fear that she wasn't quite worthy of marriage to such an interesting and successful man as Grey Hamilton. Now her fear seemed to have turned into a self-fulfilling prophecy.

She scooped loose tea leaves into the pot and poured hot water over them, stirring with desperate concentration. What, after all, did she have to offer Grey? True, she was physically attractive. She knew she must be reasonably good-looking because men had been telling her so ever since high school. She was competent at her job, and not just because of her technical skills. People who were in pain responded well to her interest and genuine sympathy, and therefore put every reserve of strength they possessed into the task of making themselves well. And she was a pretty efficient cook and housekeeper.

But that was all she could come up with on the positive side. On the negative side she acknowledged the harsh truth—that she was probably boring as hell to live with. Her parents had certainly found her dull as dishwater, greeting her achievements in high school and college with absentminded smiles and casual, uninterested words of praise. Once she had purposely brought home a report card full of C's and D's, just to see what they would say.

Her mother had glanced at it over a pile of music.

"That's nice, dear. Well done. You always do so well."

"I got three D's. If I don't do better in the next half-semester, I won't get promoted."

Her mother had already misplaced the report card under her score for *La Traviata*. "You're sure to get promoted, Kristin dear. You're so clever."

Her father had come in at that moment with some urgent question about music. In their household it was only music that ever produced any sense of urgency. Kristin had left the room, her report card still buried under a sheaf of music. After that, she stopped bringing home her report cards, and her parents had never noticed the omission.

She poured out a cup of tea and forced herself to swallow a couple of sips. The trouble was, she decided, that she lacked sparkle; she lacked dramatic flair. Her mother and father both had the power to command the attention of an entire room simply by walking into it, whereas she...well, she seemed to fade into the wallpaper. When she had attended parties with them as a teenager, she had often felt invisible. Hours could pass without anybody talking to her or even noticing she was in the room.

Kristin walked over to the TV and switched it on, then switched it off again almost before the picture stabilized on the screen. She had thought the scars of her unconventional childhood had all been healed long ago, but now doubts about her self-worth returned to haunt her. Her parents had never placed any particular value on her talents. Why should she assume Grey would value her any more highly?

True, he had seemed to love her. True, they had struck sparks from each other from the moment they first met. But physical attraction, even a very intense physical attraction, wasn't love and never could be. And without real love to back it up, the physical attraction was bound to lose its appeal eventually.

For some reason the thought suddenly flashed through

her mind that the man in the restaurant—the drunken man who had mistaken Grey for somebody called Paul Mason—had claimed he'd met Grey in Washington. The memory of that strange scene lay in her mind, curiously unsettling despite its apparent irrelevance.

Kristin shook her head, bewildered by the meanderings of her own subconscious. An abrupt flare of anger erupted deep inside her, jolting her out of her mood of self-pity. She tossed the dregs of the tea into the sink and stormed out of the kitchen. Why was she blaming herself for the failure of their marriage? Most marriages ran into trouble at some time or another. If she and Grey had problems, she was prepared to work at them. But Grey, apparently, wanted to cut and run at the first hint of difficulty.

Why had she been reproaching herself? she thought, feeling the invigorating rush of fury course through her veins. Grey had made wonderful, secret vows of love to her when they first agreed to get married. He had made public vows of loyalty and commitment at their wedding ceremony. Surely she had the right to expect those vows to last a little longer than a year.

She stripped off her clothes and stood under the stinging spray of the shower. If she ever found out who that other woman was, she would probably murder her. And when Grey came home, she was going to nail his hide to the bedroom wall. Not probably. For sure.

Chapter Four

KRISTIN FILLED THE long hours of an empty Saturday by spending all of October's housekeeping money in Denver's most expensive shopping mall. She ate lunch at a patisserie, blowing the month's entire calorie allowance with the same abandon that she had squandered the housekeeping funds. As a trainee physiotherapist, she had been required to take several psychology courses, and, at one level of her mind, she recognized exactly what she was doing. Nevertheless, these activities helped to block out the pain sufficiently to get her through the day. While she was out among the busy Saturday shoppers, she could forget the emptiness of the apartment even if she couldn't quite forget about Grey.

When the stores closed, she had no choice but to go home. She drove slowly through the darkening streets and walked reluctantly into the kitchen, dumping her

41

packages on the kitchen table. The phone started to ring before she could open the first parcel. Hesitantly, of two minds as to whether or not she should answer, she reached out and picked it up.

"Hi, sweetheart, I'm glad I found you in! I was afraid you might be out carousing around the town with some handsome doctor!"

"Hello, Grey," she said. She thought that her voice sounded astonishingly normal, although she was shaking so badly she was afraid the phone might drop out of her hand.

"How's things, honey? Did you have a good day?"

"Oh, so-so." She drew in a deep breath, scared that if she lost her temper she might say terrible things she would regret later. A long-distance phone call wasn't the right way to discuss what she had seen at the airport. "Yes, I had a good day," she said. "I spent a lot of money."

Grey sighed. "I should have known you'd be up to no good the minute my back was turned. And to think I hoped you might have had a change of heart. I thought you might be planning to surprise me."

She nearly choked. "S-surprise you?"

"By painting the bathroom." Grey's voice deepened. "Kristin, are you all right, honey? Has something happened? You sound—miserable."

"I'm fine. I'm positively wonderful. Never been better." With a supreme effort, she cut off the flow of sarcasm. She wanted to scream out her hurt, hurl wild, bitter accusations, but some lingering remnant of rationality kept her anger in check. "Where are you calling from, Grey?"

"The hotel. I just came up to my room to change."

"Which hotel?"

"Honestly, Kristin, you're hopeless. I left the name and number tacked onto the refrigerator door. What if there'd been an emergency. How would you have reached me?"

"I suppose I'd have managed." Kristin swallowed hard and carried the phone over to the fridge. Sure enough, Grey had used a magnet to pin an efficient, typewritten copy of his itinerary to the door. His secretary, like his wife, apparently thought he was spending the weekend at a science convention in Buffalo. "I have the number now," she said.

Not managing to sound as casual as she would have liked, she asked, "Is this hotel where you're staying the same place the convention is being held?"

"Of course it is, honey." Grey sounded faintly impatient. "You know what these conventions are like. Everybody gets booked into the same hotel so the organizers can keep the schedule tight."

"Oh, I see." Her hand clenched into a fist around the receiver. "Are you alone? Or are you . . . are you sharing a room?"

"I'm alone, thank heaven. Although Professor Aken is right next door, and he keeps finding something urgent to discuss with me at regular five-minute intervals. I'm surprised he hasn't been pounding on the door while I've been talking to you."

"We got lucky, I guess."

"I guess. Honey, I have to go. I want to squeeze in a shower before dinner. There's a formal banquet tonight, and you know what that means: three hours of boring speeches while we all eat tasteless carrots and overcooked chicken. Lord, sometimes these things are a drag! I wish we were up in the mountains together, admiring the aspen leaves."

He sounded so sincere that for a moment hope flared. Surely he couldn't say such things if he had a woman— that woman—lying next to him.

She was silent for a long time. "It's lonely here without you," she said at last.

"Not half as lonely as it is here," he responded gruffly. "I've been traveling far too much lately, and I'm tired of it."

She was searching for the right words to express some of the turmoil she was feeling when he spoke again. "Honey, the fact is, I have some bad news. I won't be home tomorrow night like we planned."

She closed her eyes, shutting in the sudden tears. "That's unexpected, isn't it?"

"Yes. Bill Aken's paper caused so much interest that they want to hold a special seminar on Monday morning to discuss it. There wasn't time to answer all the relevant questions this afternoon. Bill's asked me to stay over, and, of course, I can't refuse. In any case, it looks like being an interesting meeting with some first-rate people, and I'd like to stay."

"I'm sure you would," she said, not believing a word of his excuses.

"Hey, Kris, do I detect a note of sarcasm there? Honey, are you *sure* you're all right? You don't sound like you usually do."

"I'm fine. I told you I'm fine."

"I'm not convinced, honey. You sound really down. Anyway, take care of yourself until I get home, and then we'll see what I can do to console you. I have two days to dream up something spectacular." His voice deepened into tenderness. "I love you, Kris. Did I remember to tell you that recently?"

She was so angry she was afraid she was going to be sick. For a moment she thought she was going to throw up right where she stood. She leaned against the wall, needing the support.

"I'll see you Monday night, Grey," she said, and hung up quickly before he could tell her any more lies.

She was still leaning against the wall, shaking with pain and suppressed fury, when there was a buzz on the apartment's intercom. Automatically, scarcely conscious of what she was doing, Kristin depressed the speaker button. "Hello?"

"I have to talk to Paul. Tell him it's important, okay?"

Her heart stopped beating, then raced forward in a

sudden, accelerated rhythm. She cleared her throat. "You want to speak to Paul? Paul who?"

"Paul Mason."

Her heart performed a repeat of its previous lurch. She waited until she could breathe normally before she spoke. "What's your name?"

There was a pause. "Tell Paul that Damon's here, okay? Tell him I have to see him, but I'll only take a few minutes of his time."

Kristin detected a trace of a foreign accent when the man spoke, and, even over the crackle of static on the intercom, she had no difficulty in deducing that the caller, whoever he might be, was very nervous. With only a passing thought for the potential danger of what she was doing, she pressed the button that controlled the electronic lock on the doors into the building.

"You can come up," she said. "Our apartment is on the left when you leave the elevator."

She walked into the living room, vaguely aware that she was in a state of shock. She guessed that her nervous system had suffered an overload, which was probably why she felt no particular emotion as she waited for the man called Damon to arrive at the door. Her mind remained blank and her body numb until the doorbell buzzed and jerked her into action.

She opened the door, leaving the chain in place, and scrutinized her visitor. He was young, thin, and obviously jumpy. He wore a shabby suit, a dark blue shirt, and a bright red tie. He held his hands up in the air, as if to indicate that he concealed no weapons, and he looked over his shoulder three times during the brief time it took Kristin to inspect him. Altogether, she concluded, he was exactly the sort of undesirable character no woman in her right mind would let into her apartment.

She disengaged the chain, excusing herself mentally by pretending that what she was doing was more sensible than it appeared. Two people had identified Grey as Paul Mason within the space of a few days, and she wanted to know why. She cast one final glance at the man on her doorstep. He appeared as shifty and undesirable as he had at first. She drew in a deep breath.

"Come in," she said.

He slid inside the door and walked toward the center of the living room, standing there on the balls of his feet as if poised for immediate flight.

"Won't you sit down?" she asked.

"I'm okay. I'll stand. Okay if I smoke?" He didn't wait for her to answer, but pulled a pack of cigarettes from his pocket and lit up with the swift efficiency of a chain-smoker. He took a couple of deep drags. "Okay if I speak to Paul now?"

Kristin clasped her hands behind her back so that the man wouldn't see they were shaking. "What do you want to see him . . . Paul . . . about?"

"Personal business, lady."

"How did you know Paul lives here? His name isn't on the directory downstairs."

For a moment she thought the man wasn't going to answer her, then he shrugged. "I followed him. Saw him on University Boulevard last week, and so I followed him home. Okay?"

"Why didn't you just go up to him and tell him whatever's on your mind?"

Damon's expression was incredulous, then he shrugged again in a distinctly European gesture of dismissal. "Look, lady, I have things to discuss with Paul. Private, personal things. Are you gonna get him for me or are you gonna stand there all night asking stupid questions?"

"Paul isn't here," Kristin finally admitted. "But I can take a message for him if you like."

"Sure." Damon laughed nervously, lighting another cigarette from the stub of his previous one. "Thanks a lot, lady."

To Kristin's horror, he pushed past her and walked down the hallway, flinging open doors to inspect the rooms behind them. He even slid open the closet doors and rifled quickly, professionally, through the contents. She trotted after him, murmuring useless protests, until he returned to the front door. She noticed that for some reason he now looked more nervous than ever.

He stopped in the act of opening the apartment door, and turned to confront her with his hand still poised over the safety catch. "Maybe I do have a message for Paul, after all. Tell him to watch out. They're onto his ass as well as mine. I've seen them, okay? And if you're wise, lady, you won't let no more people into the apartment when Paul isn't home. That's a crazy thing to do, lady, okay?"

He slipped through the front door, closing it quietly behind him. All that was left to remind Kristin of his presence was a lingering smell of stale smoke—and a growing sense of paranoia. She quickly locked and bolted the door.

With a sudden return of the sense of humor that had been sadly lacking over the past two days, she decided to make a pot of coffee first and save her hysterics for afterward. She brewed the coffee, then sat down at the kitchen table, cupping her hands around the mug and trying to make sense of the encounter with Damon.

She wondered if he was a criminal on the run from the police. He had looked and sounded exactly as she imagined a small-time crook would look and sound. Of course, she had never previously met a crook of any variety, so her impression wasn't exactly based on first-hand experience. Nevertheless, she'd watched as many cops-and-robbers shows as anybody else, and Damon had looked like a man sent out by central casting to audition for the part of the bad guy.

She sipped her coffee as wild, unfocused images of Grey in the role of master criminal stirred in her mind. She tried to visualize him as the leader of a mysterious gang of thieves and thugs, on the run from the Mafia, but it was impossible to make the visions jell into a realistic picture. Maybe she didn't know Grey as well as she ought to, maybe there were important parts of his character he had kept hidden from her, but she would still stake her own life—literally—on the fact that he was not involved in any form of criminal activity. The rock-hard, uncompromising integrity of his character had been one of the traits that first drew her to him.

She wandered into the living room and flipped on the television set, watching fixedly until the credits of the late-late movie rolled across the screen. She switched off the set, realizing she had almost no idea what she had seen because her thoughts had been so confused and full of Grey.

She got ready for bed, still feeling almost too bewildered to be miserable. Her confusion was so great that it left no room for other emotions. If Grey was having an affair with another woman, he was certainly going to extraordinary lengths to cover his tracks. Was he really the sort of man who would create an entirely separate identity simply to cover up an affair? Up until two days ago, she would have sworn that, if he no longer loved her, he would have had the courage and honesty to tell her so.

And yet, whether he was having an affair or not, it was clear that he hadn't been honest with her recently. Thinking back over the past couple of months, Kristin reached the painful conclusion that Grey probably had been lying to her consistently. She refused to believe it was merely a wild coincidence that two apparently unconnected people had identified him as the mysterious Paul Mason. Furthermore, now that she thought back, she could remember a trail of mysterious phone conversations, cut off abruptly when she entered the room—phone conversations, moreover, that had started just about the same time that Grey's travel schedule had unexpectedly increased. And his resistance to the idea of starting their family had begun just after he'd taken his first "unexpected" business trip.

The more she thought, the less clear everything became. The conclusion that seemed ironclad one moment seemed completely untenable the next. The night gave every appearance of being endless, but just before dawn it occurred to Kristin that, since Grey's trips were supposedly caused by pressing university business, his secretary ought to know about all of them. Sue worked not only for Grey, but also for Professor Aken. She would know whether the professor had been scheduled to present a paper in Buffalo this weekend, and she would certainly know whether Grey had planned to attend the same conference. Although she and Sue weren't close friends, they had met occasionally for lunch. It was, Kristin decided, high time for them to get together again.

Although horribly embarrassed by her own deviousness, she remained firm in her decision. First thing on Monday morning she telephoned Grey's office and, doing her best to sound friendly and casual when, in fact, she felt tense and vaguely hostile, she set up a luncheon date for noon. She and Sue agreed to meet in a Mexican restaurant halfway between the hospital and the university.

Sue greeted her with such open friendliness that Kristin's guilt immediately increased two hundred percent. She covered it with a warm smile and inquired with real interest about Sue's two teenage sons.

"Chris is making straight A's like he always does, and he's just made the basketball team, so he's over the moon. And Ron's finally been accepted as a freshman at the University of Colorado in Boulder for next semester. He never did a stroke of work in high school, so he had to go to the local community college for a while, you know, to get his grades up."

"That's terrific, Sue. You must be pleased. Ron, too."

Sue grimaced. "He's pleased, but not for the right reasons. I swear the only things that kid thinks about are skiing and girls, not necessarily in that order. Whenever I ask him what courses he's planning on taking, he says it's too early to think about that and goes back to polishing his ski poles. That's on those rare occasions when I see him long enough to ask a question. Usually all I see is the flash of my car keys disappearing out the back door."

Kristin took this tale of parental woe with a pinch of salt. "You know you think Ron's terrific. You turn pink with pride every time you mention his name."

Sue looked smug. "Well, you have to admit he's just about the handsomest nineteen-year-old you ever laid eyes on."

Kristin laughed. "I think Chris is catching up fast."

Sue reached into the depths of her purse. "Well, since you mentioned it, I just happen to have a recent picture of Chris." She handed the snapshot across the table, and Kristin made appropriately admiring noises. Sue's sons really were exceptionally good-looking.

She passed the picture back and bit into a cheese-filled nacho in an effort to keep her manner suitably casual. "I'm glad we could meet today, Sue. I thought it might be a good time for you—I thought you wouldn't be too busy."

"Because Grey and the professor are both in Buffalo, you mean? Yes, it's a bit less hectic than usual, although Professor Aken is working on a new college textbook, so there's always a pile of typing waiting for me."

Kristin felt her body slump in a great wash of relief. Until Sue confirmed the reality of the conference, she hadn't known just how desperately she wanted to hear that there was one.

"Grey called me on Saturday night," she said, still trying to sound offhand and suspecting that she was failing miserably. Acting, she decided, was definitely not one of her major talents. "The professor's paper seems to have been a great success. Grey said the conference organizers decided to put on a special seminar just to discuss his ideas."

"Yes." Sue glanced at her watch. "They'll probably

be wrapping up the seminar just about now. They should
be home in time for an early dinner."

Kristin looked out of the restaurant window into the
sun-drenched parking lot. There was no way she could
think of to make her next question sound anything but
strange. "Er...Sue. Um...for this conference, did you
book Grey's plane ticket to Buffalo?"

"Yes, of course. I make all the travel arrangements
for people in Professor Aken's department. It's easier
for me to coordinate the travel vouchers for their expense
accounts."

"Yes, I can understand that." Kristin discovered some
spilled grains of salt on the table and devoted her attention
to scooping them into a neat pile. She cleared her throat.
"Sue, was there another geology conference this weekend? Maybe in Washington? Did Grey...er...mention
to you that he might go to Washington on the way to
Buffalo?"

For a split second there was total silence at their table.
"To Washington?" Sue said quickly. "Why do you think
Grey went there?"

Kristin's palms were damp, and she could feel her
cheeks burning. She was so embarrassed by her own
questions that, for a moment, she didn't notice the un-
characteristic vagueness of Sue's reply. She tried to think
of a lie that might sound even a little bit convincing,
then abandoned the attempt. Lying, like acting, obviously wasn't one of her talents. God, how she hated
checking up on her husband behind his back! But she
felt compelled to go on.

"I saw him at the airport," she said, and felt sure her
face had turned a shade between puce and purple. She
reached for her glass of water and gulped down several
mouthfuls.

Sue tactfully refrained from asking what Kristin had
been doing at the airport. In fact, she tactfully refrained
from asking anything. She smiled with ambiguous reassurance. "Oh, well, if you actually saw him at the

airport, I suppose he must have been going to Washington. Our department has a lot of dealings with the government, you know, what with the work that's being done on shale oil refinement and all. Professor Aken and Grey both act as consultants on government projects from time to time. Maybe he squeezed in a meeting with some government scientist on his way to Buffalo." Sue reached out and touched Kristin's hand. "Grey went to Buffalo this weekend, Kris. I promise you."

Kristin was squirming with embarrassment. She pushed back the sleeve of her sweater and glanced down. "Oh, Lord, look at the time! We'd better get the check fast. I have patients already lined up and waiting for me."

"Kristin," Sue said gently, "you're not wearing a watch."

If she blushed any more deeply, Kristin thought, she was going to burst a blood vessel. "I'm sorry," she mumbled. "But I really do have a tight schedule this afternoon."

Sue's smile was friendly. "And the professor would certainly like to find a new chapter waiting for him to proofread when he gets back." She stood up and signaled to their waitress. As she rummaged around in her purse for change, she seemed to hover on the brink of some confidence. But in the end she merely pulled on her sweater and walked briskly to the cash register.

Kristin was back at the hospital swimming in the heated pool with Missy Gordon before she was able to pin down precisely what was bothering her about her lunch date with Grey's secretary. At the time, she had been so grateful for Sue's tactful avoidance of several embarrassing questions that she hadn't registered how strangely irresolute Sue's manner had been.

Maybe the events of the past few days had finally given her an advanced case of paranoia, Kristin thought, but she was suddenly convinced that it was the questions Sue *hadn't* asked that were the really significant part of their lunchtime conversation. It seemed to her that Grey's secretary knew far too many things about his activities that Kristin *didn't* know.

She was filled with renewed impatience for Grey to return home. She still had every intention of nailing his hide to the bedroom wall. But first she was going to find time to ask him some very interesting questions.

Chapter Five

KRISTIN OPENED A bottle of imported white burgundy, put candles on the table in the dining alcove, and set two places with fancy quilted place mats. She wasn't quite sure what she was aiming to achieve, but she knew she was going to put up a fight before handing Grey over to any dark-haired beauty with spaniel eyes and a nonexistent bosom.

She was showered, perfumed, and clad in slinky black satin lounging pajamas when she heard the sound of Grey's key in the front door. She took an inelegantly large gulp of wine and propped herself against the kitchen counter, trying to look both casual and sexy. Her acting ability being as limited as it was, she wasn't too optimistic about her success.

Grey stepped briskly into the apartment, his eyes lighting up with pleasure when he saw her. She was surprised at how badly she wanted to throw herself into his arms. She deliberately held herself back, and, when she looked at him more closely, she could see a hint of some other, more complex emotion hidden behind the pleasure. She couldn't decide what that emotion was. She didn't think it was guilt, despite the quantity of lies he had recently told her.

"Hi, honey. Mmm... it's good to be home." His manner was as relaxed and intimate as ever, which scared the living daylights out of her. How many other times had he left her with a lie, then greeted her with a warm, affectionate hug when he returned?

He leaned forward to kiss her, but she twisted away, not sure she was ready to receive his embrace, not when there was so much deceit lying unresolved between them. To her astonishment, as she jerked her head to one side her gaze was drawn to the front door, and she realized that Grey hadn't come home alone. A tall blond man stood in the doorway, obviously waiting for her invitation before he stepped into the apartment.

Kristin hurriedly pulled herself out of Grey's arms, clutching ineffectually at the narrow front panels of her satin top. Nature had provided her with a generous endowment of bosom, unlike the woman at the airport, and she had chosen her outfit precisely because it displayed a fair amount of nature's bounty. What's more, the visitor's appreciative smile made it clear he thoroughly enjoyed her choice of clothing. She felt herself flush with a mixture of indignation and embarrassment.

"Grey," she said sharply, more sharply than she'd intended, "you didn't tell me you were bringing home a visitor."

Grey turned around and gestured to his friend. "Oh, Steve, come on in. I didn't realize you were waiting outside."

He swung back and gave Kristin an apologetic grin. "I had no chance to call you, honey. It was all decided at the last minute, but I knew you wouldn't mind. You're always so well prepared. Kristin, this is Steve Callahan, an old friend from way back. We ran into each other at the conference in Buffalo, and he has business in Denver tomorrow, so I invited him to stay with us. Steve, this is my wife."

Grey beamed proudly as he propelled Kristin forward to shake Steve's hand. Just as if he had the clearest conscience in the world, she thought angrily. Just as if he hadn't parted from her with a lie and spent Friday evening, if not the whole weekend, with another woman. Either he was really proud of her, or he was the world's best actor or... or what? She couldn't come up with any other satisfactory alternative to her own question.

At any other time she would have welcomed the chance to meet one of Grey's friends, but tonight she definitely wasn't in the mood to be sociable to total strangers. She had to quell a feeling of resentment as Steve Callahan crossed the tiny hallway and joined them in the kitchen. It wasn't his fault, she reminded herself, that he had walked in on a major marital row. A marital row, she realized with a rueful appreciation of the absurdities, where she was the only partner who knew they were fighting.

Steve's manner remained relaxed, even though, for some reason, she was sure he sensed her inner tension. She noticed that he was polite enough, once inside the front door, to keep his gaze tactfully averted from her inadequate satin halter, and she was grateful for his courtesy.

She held out her hand to return his handshake and experienced a strange ripple of awareness when her eyes met his. He radiated a power and self-confidence combined with a sexuality that was all the more potent for being, she was sure, entirely unconscious. She realized with a jolt of surprise that, apart from movie stars and sports heroes, she could think of only two other men who possessed that same sort of dynamic inner power: her father... and Grey.

She had no time to pursue the thought. Steve said hello and held out a large, silver-wrapped package, smiling as he handed it to her. "Grey insisted you wouldn't mind me spending the night," he said. "But as a man who's learned a great deal in two years of marriage, I know better. I'm smart enough to know I have to offer abject apologies for intruding. My wife says I have a fail-safe system: I only bring home unexpected guests on days when she's totally exhausted and planning to serve two-day-old leftovers for dinner. I hope Grey doesn't discover he's working on the same system."

Kristin's answering smile wasn't as warm as she would have liked. It was so frustrating to be forced to delay the confrontation with her husband. "You aren't intruding," she said stiffly. "Grey's friends are always welcome."

Steve's smile changed to an outright grin. "I'll come clean and admit the truth, Kristin. This gift is a bribe, to make sure I don't get thrown out onto the street before Grey and I have a chance to catch up on old times."

It was difficult to resist his charm. Her smile was more genuine as she murmured her thanks and began to unwrap the heavy package. "Were you and Grey at college together?" she asked, making amends for her earlier hostility.

There was a fractional pause. "We attended the same graduate school," Steve said. "But I'm a nuclear physicist by training, and Grey, of course, is a mining engineer."

"I didn't know the Colorado School of Mines trained physicists."

"Actually, we weren't together at the School of Mines," Steve said smoothly. "We met in Washington after Grey graduated from there."

"In Washington?"

"Yes. At—er—Georgetown University, in fact."

Kristin glanced at her husband in surprise. "I never knew you went to Georgetown, Grey. I didn't even know you'd spent time in Washington."

It seemed to her that, for a split second, his fingers

tightened against her arm. "I'm sure I must have mentioned it, Kris. It's not like me to hide any of my successes. I worked for the federal government when I first got out of school, you know. Lots of young scientists do."

The glance he threw in Steve Callahan's direction seemed entirely casual. Kristin had no idea why she suddenly suspected it was loaded with hidden meaning.

"You'd better be careful what you say, old friend." Grey's manner was disarmingly humorous as he thumped Steve on the shoulder. "Don't go dredging up too many stories about our days together as students. Remember I'm a married man nowadays—and I'd like to stay that way!"

"As an old married man myself, I can assure you I've already learned the dangers of too much reminiscing."

The men laughed heartily as Kristin removed the last of the wrapping from Steve's present and revealed a tastefully arranged gift box of fresh fruit and cheese, intermingled with foil-wrapped chocolates.

"Why, thank you, Steve, what a thoughtful gift! We'll eat the strawberries with some ice cream for dessert, and have some of the chocolates with our after-dinner coffee."

"That sounds like a great idea," Grey said. "Oh, boy! Ice cream and chocolate all in one day. It must be my birthday!" He grinned in Steve's direction. "Kristin is always on a diet so, for some strange reason, *I'm* never allowed to eat dessert. Recently I've noticed that I start to salivate every time I pass the candy machine at the office. But my wife has me so psyched out about the dangers of junk food that I'm afraid to stop and buy one."

They all laughed, although Kristin was aware of a strange undercurrent of tension that seemed to vibrate in the air around her. She forced herself to meet Steve Callahan's eyes for the second time and was disconcerted to find them examining her with a cool intensity that seemed out of place in such a casual visitor. She put the gift box down on the kitchen counter, pleased when she managed to speak with a great deal more self-possession than she felt.

"If you two will excuse me, I'm going to change into something a bit warmer. It seems to have turned a little chilly, don't you think? Grey, do you want to fix Steve a drink while I find something else to wear? Or maybe you could show him the guest room?"

"Sure. How about dinner? Can I do anything to help?"

"Shred a few extra lettuce leaves and slice another tomato for the salad. I'm sure Steve will understand that I wasn't expecting visitors."

There was an acid note in her voice that she immediately regretted. She really was becoming paranoid, for heaven's sake. She was allowing her uncertainties about Grey to spill over into suspicions about this perfectly innocent houseguest, who merely wanted the chance to talk over old times with his college friend. As she changed into tailored slacks and a simple silk blouse, she resolved that she would be more hospitable to Steve Callahan over dinner.

She emerged from the bedroom to find the two men nursing drinks and laughing over some highly colored story about a raid they had led on a sorority house during their stay at Georgetown.

She accepted a glass of white wine from Grey, then went into the kitchen to check on the scallops, which were already simmering in the oven. She couldn't help smiling as she added another place setting to the table and listened to the men swap increasingly outrageous stories. It was hard to remain angry with Grey as she heard him recall the triumph of some nocturnal excursion into the girls' dorm—and the horrors of the morning after in the dean's office.

"I can't believe you two were still behaving like overgrown adolescents when you were postgraduates," she said when she went to tell them dinner was ready. Her smile removed all the sting from her words.

Grey hugged her as he rose to his feet. "Honey, if there are a bunch of women locked up somewhere officially out-of-bounds, you can bet all the red-blooded males in the vicinity are immediately going to revert to an aggressive state of adolescence."

"The old instinct that compels men to invade the harem," Steve agreed. "Even though they know what will happen if the sultan finds out." They moved to the dining room alcove and he held out a chair for Kristin. "You know," he said as she began to serve the food, "sometimes I feel sorry for college kids today. There are no silly rules left for them to break, so how do they let off steam when they need to relax for a while? If I were a college president, I think I'd introduce a few unnecessary rules so that the student body could get together and protest them. Hell, half the fun of college used to be doing the things you knew you weren't supposed to be doing. Nowadays there's no curfew, so you can't work off excess energy climbing in your window after hours. You can't stage a raid on the girls' dorm, because all the dorms are coed, and anyway most of the girls would be sleeping with their boyfriends. What's left to do when you feel a bit reckless?"

"Get drunk," Kristin said grimly.

"Or get high," Grey added. "Kristin spends a lot of time reconstructing the smashed-up bodies of kids who thought they could drive when they were drunk. Or when they were high. Or sometimes when they were both."

"No," Kristin said tersely. "The ones who try drugs and alcohol together don't usually come to me. They end up in the mortuary."

"That must be one of the toughest parts of your profession," Steve said quietly. "But, in fact, I don't think student drinking is a new problem. I seem to remember we got drunk regularly when we were in college, even though we had so many other, more sensible ways to let off steam. Sometimes, now that I'm getting old, I think it's a miracle the human race ever makes it through adolescence."

"Now that you're getting old," Grey exclaimed. "Hey, when did that happen? I thought you were the same age as me."

"I aged a generation in twenty-four hours the day our daughter was born," Steve said. He laughed, but there was an undercurrent of seriousness to his words. "There's nothing like becoming a father for making you realize just how precarious life is and how desperately vulnerable children can be. I looked at my baby daughter lying in that hospital crib, so perfect and so helpless, and I realized I was absolutely terrified. Sometimes I think women cope more easily with becoming mothers than men cope with becoming fathers. Megan adores Stephanie, yet she seems to take everything pretty much in stride. I was shaking the first time she asked me to hold the baby."

For a moment Kristin's attention was concentrated totally on Steve. She was fascinated by this glimpse into his character. He must be basically a very confident man, she thought, to express his vulnerability with such frankness. She glanced at Grey, wondering how he was reacting to the conversation, and she saw that his face had turned white beneath its tan. Then the impression of pallor vanished as he gave a mock groan.

"Oh, no! How did we manage to do this to ourselves, Kris. Steve and Megan have just become parents, and at the merest thread of an excuse he produces about two hundred candid snapshots of baby Stephanie. Are you ready to spend the rest of the evening cooing over baby pictures?"

"Of course! You know how much I love children. How old is your daughter, Steve?"

"Three and a half months." Steve scowled at Grey, feigning offense. "And you're quite wrong about the two hundred pictures. I only have two."

"What happened to the other hundred and ninety-eight?" Grey teased. "Did Megan confiscate them?"

"I would love to see the pictures," Kristin said, smiling as Steve willingly pulled a leather folder out of his jacket pocket and passed it to her. She examined the two color shots. They showed a chubby, smiling infant with a fluff of blond curls and wide gray eyes.

"She's adorable, but I don't think she looks like you," she said, "although her coloring is similar."

Steve returned the pictures to his pocket. "No, she looks like my wife, Megan. She's a very good baby, always laughing."

Steve's expression normally was hard and somewhat controlled. It softened, Kristin noticed, every time he spoke his wife's name. She felt a tight ache in the pit of her stomach and wondered if Grey's face ever held that wistful, loving look when he talked about her to strangers.

"Well, are you two ready for dessert?" she asked with forced cheerfulness. "Thanks to you, Steve, I can offer cheese as well as strawberries and chocolate."

Not surprisingly, Grey elected to have strawberries, ice cream, *and* chocolate. "A lot of all of them, please."

Steve requested cheese. "I've been eating too many rich desserts lately," he said. "I've come to the conclusion that all my pants can't be shrinking at the dry cleaner."

"Was the food good at the conference?" Kris asked, arranging a plate of cheese and crackers and a bowl of strawberries in the center of the table.

"Not bad. You know what it's like when you're catering for a mob."

"How many people were actually there this weekend?"

"Must have been more than a thousand," Grey said. "I never knew there were so many geologists and mining engineers with time on their hands to come and listen to lectures."

"What were you doing at a mining conference, Steve?" Kristin asked, more out of politeness than any genuine curiosity. She had long ago accepted the fact that Grey really had been in Buffalo over the weekend, even if he had spent Friday night somewhere in Washington. She didn't doubt for a moment that Grey and Steve Callahan actually had met at the conference.

"Oh, I only attended the odd session that seemed relevant to my field," Steve said. "Unlike Grey, I didn't have to sit through all the lectures."

"With a thousand people at the convention center, it was lucky you happened to meet up," she said. "Or did you both know in advance that the other guy was going to be there?"

"It was really an odd coincidence," Steve replied with a little laugh. "We happened to get lucky. I was working in Denver last Friday, and I ran into Grey at the airport. We discovered we were taking the same flight to the conference, so we flew into Buffalo together."

Kristin had a spoonful of ice cream in her mouth. She was amazed that she managed to swallow it. She was even more amazed that she managed to continue breathing normally so that, when she spoke, her voice sounded entirely natural. "You flew into Buffalo together?" she asked. "On Friday night?"

"Yes." Steve's smile never wavered. He looked as honest and sincere as he always had. "It's a four-hour flight, you know, so it was good to have an old friend to talk to."

"It must have been. I don't suppose you have many chances to get together."

"No," Grey interjected, his smile as open and as honest-looking as Steve's. "We hardly ever see each other nowadays. Steve still works for the government, so he's headquartered in Washington."

"Of course. And you never go there, do you, Grey?"

She pushed her chair away from the table, wondering for a frightening moment if she really might be going crazy. Nothing seemed to add up anymore. Wasn't it one of the first signs of madness when you believed that everybody around you was entering into a conspiracy to conceal the truth? How could she possibly think that

Steve Callahan was part of some complex plot to deceive her? God, the idea was insane! Maybe *she* was going insane.

"I knew I shouldn't have eaten that ice cream," she said, making the first excuse that entered her head. "Chocolate marshmallow always does me in. Steve, Grey, excuse me, please."

She hurried into the bedroom, resisting the temptation to lock the door behind her. She went into the bathroom and splashed cold water on her burning cheeks. The feeling of nausea slowly began to subside. Dammit, she wasn't crazy! She had seen Grey leave for Washington with a woman clinging to his arm. Therefore Steve couldn't have flown with Grey to Buffalo, at least not on Friday night. Therefore Steve, together with her husband, was lying through his teeth. But *why?*

Hearing Grey's footsteps approaching the bedroom, she hastily slammed the bathroom door shut, locking it and leaning against it in her determination to stop Grey from coming in. All evening she had been waiting to confront him. Now she was suddenly reluctant to voice her accusations. She was afraid of what she might hear.

"Kris, honey, are you all right?" Grey asked. His voice sounded soft with concern and tenderness. "Can I do anything to help?"

"Nothing, thank you. I'll be fine in a moment."

"Kris, was it really just the ice cream? Can't you open the door for a minute? I want to see you."

"No, I don't want to open the door." She wasn't sure if she could face Grey without screaming, but she knew for sure she couldn't look at Steve Callahan again tonight. She drew in a deep breath. "Grey, it's late, and I'm tired. Why don't you show your good old friend Steve to his room? Give him the portable TV from the kitchen, offer him a selection of books, and suggest he has an early night."

"All right, if that's what you want. Is the sofa bed made up?"

"I think so."

"Kris, this whispering through the bathroom door is ridiculous. What's going on in there?"

I'm going quietly crazy, she thought. She bit back a gasp of hysterical laughter and turned on the cold-water tap.

"I'm brushing my teeth," she said. "I'm getting rid of the taste of chocolate marshmallow."

Despite the closed door, she could almost see Grey's shrug. "I'll fix Steve up for the night, Kris, and then I think you and I have some things to talk about."

"Funny you should mention that. I was thinking pretty much the same thing."

She could feel the waves of frustration emanating from Grey's side of the door. She was still shaking when she heard him call Steve's name. She listened in taut silence to the clatter of their progress down the narrow hallway. Their voices faded as they reached the paneled den that also served as a guest bedroom. Somebody, presumably, had closed the den door.

She emerged from the bathroom and hurried into the kitchen. Most of the dishes had already been stacked in the dishwasher. She hurriedly cleared away the final few remains of their dinner, shoving leftovers into the fridge with none of her usual neatness. She wanted to be out of the kitchen quickly in case Steve came into the living room for some reason.

She was hurrying back into the bedroom when she remembered that there was no pillow on the spare bed. She debated letting Steve sleep with only the sofa cushion to rest his head on, then her instincts as a hostess got the better of her. She retrieved the spare pillow from the top shelf of the bedroom closet, found a clean white pillowcase, and walked hesitantly toward the den. She would simply hand the pillow over, say the briefest possible good night, and return immediately to her own bedroom. The rules of hospitality didn't require her to make conversation with a man who told blatant lies, even if he was one of her husband's friends from "way back."

Steve and Grey were talking softly, their voices so low and muted that it wasn't until she was right outside the door that she heard the anger vibrating in Grey's words. Her hand hovered over the mock-oak panels of the door, poised to knock, but her movements were arrested by shock. She had never heard such restrained violence in any man's tone, certainly had never believed Grey was capable of feeling such intensity of emotion.

"I don't give a damn if her father was born in Czechoslovakia! I don't give a damn if he had a dozen concert tours in Eastern Europe last year! We're discussing my relationship with my *wife!*"

Steve's voice was even lower than Grey's, less angry but no less intense. "It's for Kristin's own protection, Grey, and for the protection of her family. I came here at your request for a personal evaluation and, in my professional judgment, your wife isn't ready to be told."

"Screw your professional judgment! What could Kristin have done or said to prove she was ready?"

There was a tiny pause. "She could have kissed you when you walked in the door, maybe?"

Grey muttered a string of expletives, half of which Kristin didn't even recognize. Whether or not he planned to say anything more intelligible, she never discovered. She heard the sound of sudden, quick footsteps crossing the wooden floor, and she just had time to dodge a couple of feet away from the entrance before the door was jerked open.

Steve Callahan nodded in her direction. "I thought I heard somebody in the corridor," he said casually. His smile was so disarmingly friendly that she almost choked. She could scarcely believe that such an innocent face could conceal so much deception. Somehow she managed to dredge up an answering smile of her own, although she was sure it lacked Steve's dazzling appearance of sincerity.

"I brought you a pillow," she said. "I hope you find

the bed comfortable. We've only had a couple of visitors before you, but they both said they slept well."

"I'm sure it will be fine. I'm one of those lucky people who can sleep anywhere."

"That's good. Grey's like that, too." She couldn't believe they were exchanging this inane chitchat.

Grey came out of the den at that precise moment, and she saw that he, too, had resumed his mask of smiling charm. She thrust the pillow at Steve, turning away abruptly. She couldn't cope with this nonsensical scene any longer.

"Good night," she said, unable to think of anything else to add. There seemed to be no room in her mind for anything but the pitch and toss of constant confusion. She hurried down the corridor to the welcome privacy of the bedroom and waited for Grey to come to her.

Chapter Six

GREY FOLLOWED HER into the bedroom almost immediately, shutting the door firmly behind him. There were tight lines of strain around his mouth, Kristin noticed, lines she had never seen before, and his eyes held an unprecedented touch of weariness. She turned away, confused by her sudden rush of sympathy. She began to undress, pretending a great interest in the hook of her leather belt and total absorption in the simple task of unfastening her buttons.

"Kristin, will you tell me what's wrong?" Grey asked quietly.

She kept her gaze fixed on the buttons. "I'm not sure where to begin."

"How about with Saturday, when I called you from Buffalo. I knew then that something was bothering you."

She whirled around to face him. "Yet you still brought

your good old buddy, your great friend Steve Callahan, home with you. How did you expect us to discuss anything personal with him underfoot?"

"It was a mistake to bring him back with me, I realize that now. I'm sorry, but it seemed like a good idea at the time."

Why? she wondered. Why had it seemed like a good idea? Judging from the snippet of conversation she'd overheard, Steve had come here to pass some sort of professional judgment on her. What sort of evaluation had Grey asked Callahan to provide? Her mind boggled at the possible implications.

She tossed her blouse in the direction of the laundry hamper, then remembered it was pure silk and hastily picked it up again. "Why did you go to that convention, Grey?" she asked. "Was it just to meet Steve?"

Genuine astonishment shone in his eyes as he turned to look at her. "No, of course that wasn't why I went. Kris, what is this? I've already told you I went to that convention because Bill Aken was delivering a major paper, and he asked me to go with him. That can't be what's bothering you, surely. You can't be angry because I spent the weekend at a professional conference. We've always recognized the demands of each other's professions."

"No, of course that isn't what's bothering me."

"Then what is? Kristin, I've had a hell of a week, and—believe it or not—a worse weekend. I'm not in the mood to play games with you while you decide whether or not to tell me what's bugging you. And while you're mulling over my past crimes, perhaps you'd like to add a future one to your list. I have a meeting scheduled at the University of Pennsylvania on Wednesday morning. I'll have to fly out of here tomorrow night, and I don't know exactly when I'll be back. Hopefully before the weekend, but it's not certain. I'm sorry. Sometimes we can't arrange our schedules to suit our personal convenience."

"How are you flying to Philadelphia?"

"I thought about catching a plane. Do you have any better suggestions?"

"I meant what route are you planning to follow?" she asked sarcastically. "Are you going via Washington again? Or do you think you might save time and fly direct to Philadelphia?"

There wasn't even a moment's pause before Grey answered her. "Fly via Washington?" he asked, appearing genuinely puzzled. "Kris, what are you talking about?"

"I'm talking about your trip to Buffalo," she said, hearing her voice shake even though she tried to conceal the extent of her anger. "I know you went via Washington."

"Kristin, the last time I went to Washington on university business was right after we got back from our honeymoon. Bill Aken nearly always makes the reports on any federal government studies we do. That's only right; he's the senior consultant on all these projects, after all."

Kristin looked at him sadly. "You're very good at avoiding telling the truth at the same time that you don't quite tell a lie, aren't you, Grey? It's a real talent of yours."

"Do you think you could stop talking in riddles and tell me precisely what you're getting at?"

"I guess so." She turned away, staring hard at the bedpost so that she wouldn't start to cry. She didn't understand her own reactions. Anger didn't usually make her tearful. In fact, she had learned as a young child both to control her tears and to tame her emotions. But tonight her emotions refused to be controlled, and her words spilled out in a torrent of harsh, clipped sound.

"I was at Stapleton Airport on Friday afternoon, Grey. I had a big surprise all planned for you. I was going to join you in Buffalo and keep your bed warm between boring convention seminars. As it turned out, there was only one problem with my nifty little plan: You didn't fly to Buffalo. At least not on Friday afternoon. You flew to Washington and, what's more, you had another woman with you. If she'd been clinging any closer to your side, she'd have turned into a barnacle. The stewardess must have needed to scrape her off your arm to get her into her seat."

"So *that's* what's been bugging you." Grey crossed the room in swift strides, gathering her into his arms and pressing her head toward the warm, hard support of his chest. But she refused to be comforted, holding her body stiff and unyielding against him.

"Oh, sweetheart!" he said softly. "If only you'd come up and said something to me right there at the airport. Yes, I was at the Washington departure gate. Yes, there was a woman with me. But she's not my lover; she's not my mistress; she's not even a friend, not exactly." He held her away from him, forcing her to look up at him. "I swear to you, Kris, you saw me with a business colleague, not with a lover."

Her voice remained tight with suppressed emotion. "But how can you say you didn't go to Washington? You went into the boarding tunnel with her. I saw you."

"Yes, well, so I did. She had some problems with a paper she was scheduled to deliver in Washington, and I was helping her work through them. The paper was very important to her, and she was nervous about presenting it. I needed a few extra minutes to reassure her."

"She didn't look like a geologist."

He gave a slight grin. "Kris, your prejudices are showing. Not all geologists have the build of a wrestler, you know."

"But she looked as if a puff of wind would blow her away."

"Appearances are deceptive, believe me. She's a very strong and very determined woman."

Kristin pulled herself out of Grey's arms, making no effort to disguise the tartness of her tone. "I still don't think she looked like a geologist, and she didn't look much like a business colleague, either, the way she was draping herself around you."

He shrugged slightly, a touch of impatience in the gesture. "She can't help fluttering her lashes and leaning against the nearest available male. As far as she's concerned, those are practically reflex gestures, and just about as meaningless. She's one of these women who's extremely talented professionally but with no confidence in her own abilities. She likes to have a man around to cling to in moments of stress. Not very liberated, maybe, but that's the way a lot of women are, Kris. Even some of the most intelligent ones."

"You sound very convincing, Grey. But then you always do sound convincing, don't you? I'm just now beginning to realize that."

He cupped her face in his hands, tracing the outline of her features with a delicate stroke of his forefinger. "Let's stop talking about her, Kris. I swear to you I don't love her. I swear to you I've never slept with her. I've never even kissed her cheek."

She couldn't prevent a few tears of frustration from squeezing out from the corners of her tightly closed eyes and trickling down to her chin. He sounded so loving and so convincing—and she wanted so much to believe him. But his story was incredible. No rational person who had seen the way the woman behaved at the airport would accept that she considered Grey merely a professional colleague. She had clung to him as if he were her personal savior, a lifeline when she was drowning, her hope for future happiness.

"There's something else, isn't there, Kristin? I still haven't heard the whole story." With seemingly infinite tenderness, Grey wiped away her tears, then brushed a quick, gentle kiss over each of her eyelids. "Please tell me the rest of what's bothering you."

"There are so many things," she said. "So many little things that I've forced myself to ignore for weeks, but I can't ignore them any longer."

"Tell me one of them," he commanded tautly.

"Do you remember that man we saw in the restaurant? The one who thought you were Paul Mason?"

She felt the immediate stiffening of his body, but all he said was, "Yes, I remember."

"Somebody else came around here looking for Paul Mason. Somebody who said his name was Damon."

Grey moved away from her, walking quickly into the bathroom to pour himself a glass of water. It was at least a minute before he came back out again, his features set into grim, hard lines.

"Do you mean somebody called Damon actually came to this apartment?" he asked. "He came here expecting to find somebody called Paul Mason?"

"Yes. Don't you think it's a bit strange that two people have mistaken you for the same man within the last few days?"

"I think it's more than a bit strange. It's an extraordinary coincidence." He went back into the bathroom and returned the glass to its place on the counter. "How did Damon find me, do you think?" he asked without turning around.

"He wasn't looking for you," Kristin said with a deliberate lack of emphasis. "He was looking for somebody called Paul Mason."

"Dammit, you know what I meant! I meant, why did Damon come to this apartment looking for a guy named Paul?"

"He said he saw you on University Boulevard one day last week and followed you home."

Grey swung around, looking at her sharply. "Where were you talking to him? How did he have time to tell you all this?"

She flushed and dropped her gaze. "He buzzed the intercom and asked for Paul Mason. I . . . er . . . I invited him to come up."

"You what! You asked some lunatic to come up to

the apartment when you were all alone? Kris, are you trying to get yourself murdered or something?"

"No," she shouted. "I'm trying to find out what's going on around here, and it seems that you're determined not to tell me! Grey, why have two people thought you were called Paul Mason?"

His expression remained unreadable, and his voice was tight. "I should think the answer to that question is obvious. No big mystery. I must look very much like somebody called Paul Mason. And, since he's a man who doesn't seem to have very desirable friends, that's another excellent reason why you shouldn't let strangers into the apartment."

"Damon had a message for Paul," Kristin said, not directly acknowledging Grey's explanation. "He wanted Paul to know that—quote—they were onto Paul's ass as well as onto Damon's. End quote."

Grey's normally cool demeanor vanished completely. "My God, Kris, if I ever hear you've been letting strangers into the apartment again, I swear I'll murder you myself and save the weirdos a job. I'm probably lucky to come home and find you still in one piece."

The remnants of his self-control finally seemed to snap, and he pulled her down onto the bed, straddling her body so that she couldn't wriggle away. "Kris, promise me, please promise me, you'll never invite anybody you don't know up to the apartment, especially when I'm not here. It's too dangerous. There's a world of kooks out there, not to mention criminals and assorted other undesirables."

"I wouldn't be tempted to do dangerous things if you'd only be honest with me!"

His eyes darkened, and she could sense his frustration. "Kris, I love you more than I love anybody else in the world," he said quietly. "That's the ultimate truth, the final honesty. Surely nothing else matters."

He put out his hand, pinning the long strands of her

hair against the pillow so that she couldn't turn her head away. Slowly he lowered his mouth to hers, sealing her lips with a passionate kiss. The hair on his chest prickled against her breasts as he moved, and her body responded instinctively to the familiar, sensuous pleasure. She was aware of an unusual urgency in his lovemaking, a new tension in his kiss that was strangely erotic, but she resisted the impulse to return his embrace. Tonight, just for once, she wasn't going to allow him to dissolve her anger in the passion of their lovemaking. She had begged him to answer some valid questions. She had tacitly asked him to let her know what was going on in his life, and he had refused to confide in her. His rejection still hurt.

She kept her mouth tightly closed, and eventually he broke off the kiss. "What is it, Kris?" he asked harshly.

"I don't believe what you've told me," she said. "I asked you to explain some very strange goings-on, and your answers aren't convincing. They don't ring true, not one of them."

"You still think Narina is my mistress?"

"Narina?" she asked.

He was silent for a moment. "Narina is the woman you saw me with. Do you still think we're lovers?"

"I don't know. Maybe not. I don't seem to know anything anymore."

"I've told you several times that I don't love her and that she's never been my mistress," Grey said quietly. "Some things in a marriage have to be taken on faith, Kris. I promise you one more time that Narina and I have never even come close to being lovers. If you don't trust me enough to believe that, then our marriage is in big trouble."

She sat up on the bed, her eyes flashing fire. "Oh, no! You're not going to pull that one on me! I'm not accepting any guilt trip about our marriage when you're the one who's been lying!"

"I haven't been lying," he hissed through clenched

teeth. "What does it take to convince you?"

He jerked her angrily against his body. "Can you feel how much I want you? Do you still think I'm lying about the way you make me feel?"

She refused to reply, and he took her hand, guiding it to open the zipper of his pants and pressing her fingers against the hardness of his body.

"Do you think I'd want to make love to you so badly if I'd spent all weekend in bed with another woman?" he asked huskily.

"I don't know what I think anymore! The books all say that there's no connection between a man's emotions and his sexual appetite."

"Then the books must be written by idiots," he said tersely. "Or by frustrated women."

"Sexist remarks aren't going to resolve anything."

"No, but maybe this is." He grabbed her shoulders and forced her down against the pillows, his mouth fierce against her silky hair, his body hard and impatient with desire. When she tried to move away, he pulled her back, his eyes burning with some violent emotion, barely suppressed. He ripped off the rest of their clothes, kissing her lips and her throat and caressing her body until she was lost in a warm pool of mindless darkness. Within minutes her breasts arched up toward him in an ache of helpless longing.

His mouth burned against her skin, seeking out all the places that yearned for his touch. Although her mind still resisted him, her hands reached out to embrace him, and her legs twined tightly around his, inviting his possession.

He moved fractionally away from her, reaching out to flick off the bedside lamp. His face was flushed with desire, and she saw, in the last flare of light before it was extinguished, that his eyes glittered with diamond-hard triumph.

His voice was as seductive as velvet in the sudden

darkness. "Kristin," he murmured against her skin as his mouth traced a line of kisses across her breasts. "Oh God, Kristin, I want you."

The sound of his voice broke the sensual spell holding her in bondage, and she twisted her face away from his lips, angry with herself for the ease of her surrender. It seemed as if all Grey needed to do was kiss her or stroke her, and every one of her questions floated away into the mists of never-never land. But not tonight, she reminded herself. Tonight she had sworn she wouldn't allow herself to be carried away by the pleasures of his lovemaking. There were some problems in their marriage that couldn't be resolved by sex or passion.

"Please stop, Grey," she said. "Please! I don't want to make love tonight."

His voice was thick, and she could feel his heart throbbing urgently against her naked skin. "Let me persuade you to change your mind," he said. "Relax, and you'll find I'm a very convincing persuader."

His tongue touched her nipple, sending a spark of electricity spiraling through her body. At the same time his hand slid down to coax her thighs apart, turning her bones to liquid and her blood to fire as he gently stroked her.

It required all the willpower she possessed to thrust his hand away and roll over on the bed, out of reach of his kisses. "No, Grey. I said no!" She sounded fierce in her denial because she wasn't at all sure she could resist him. She wasn't even entirely sure she wanted to. Her reason said that sex would solve nothing, but her body pulsed with the rhythm of awakened physical need, and her breath came in short, sharp bursts.

Grey's breathing was as ragged as hers, but his voice was suddenly under complete control. "What are you doing, Kristin?" he asked sardonically. "Punishing me for my supposed sins?"

"No! Can't you understand I'm just not in the mood?"

"Not in the mood?" He reached out, casually tossing

the long strands of hair away from her throat. His fingers brushed lightly across her breasts, then traveled down her stomach and poised tantalizingly at the intersection of her thighs. Her body convulsed in an involuntary quiver of longing.

"I'm sorry you're not in the mood," he said mockingly, just as if he hadn't felt her responsive shiver. "I'm sorry I've been misreading your body language. I'm not usually so insensitive."

He removed his hand and rolled over onto his side, sliding underneath the covers so that no part of his body remained in contact with hers. He yawned. "I guess I'm bushed, after all. I could use a decent night's sleep. Good night, Kristin."

"Good night."

Silence descended on the bedroom, broken only by the soft sounds of their breathing. Kristin couldn't believe what she had done to herself. She lay in the darkness, watching the regular rise and fall of Grey's chest as his breathing gradually deepened into the rhythm of sleep.

So much for his passionate need, she thought bitterly. It must have taken him all of ten minutes to fall asleep. He hadn't even shifted position. In contrast to his state of relaxation, her body felt as if it was composed of approximately two million jangling nerve endings, all two million of them longing for Grey's touch.

She tossed restlessly on their queen-sized mattress, which seemed suddenly to be composed entirely of lumps. She was too hot, so she threw off the covers. Almost immediately she was too cold. She turned over from one side to the other and found herself facing Grey's back. Even his spine looked relaxed, she thought resentfully. *He* was the one who'd caused all the trouble, and he was sleeping peacefully while she burned up with sexual frustration.

Against her better judgment she stretched out her hand, longing to stroke her fingers down the firm, muscled line of his back. She wanted so much to be held in his arms, to see his mouth quirk into its teasing smile, to see his eyes darken with the fire of passion. She jerked her hand away from temptation, before the demands of her body could betray her common sense. It was humiliating enough that Grey could so easily arouse her to passion. It would be intolerable if—after all her angry denials—she had to admit that she ached for him to make love to her.

She sighed, closing her eyes and twisting away from the enticement of his muscled body. If she counted sheep, surely she would fall asleep eventually.

She managed to drag her thoughts away from her husband long enough to visualize a plump black sheep, with short legs and a long nose. For some reason the poor animal appeared distinctly cross-eyed. She pictured it jumping over an old-fashioned gate in a hedge of flowering honeysuckle. She had three hundred and seventy-nine black sheep lined up in the meadow before she gave up and went into the kitchen for an aspirin and a glass of milk. She noticed a crack of light under Steve Callahan's door and hoped childishly that he was suffering from a case of insomnia at least as bad as her own.

When she returned to the bedroom, Grey didn't appear to have moved. His dark eyelashes rested serenely against the tanned skin of his cheek. His forehead remained unfurrowed by any trace of worry.

She scowled ferociously and crawled under the covers. Damn the man, anyway!

She lay on her side, continuing to count sheep. This time she counted thin white ones instead of plump black ones. Four hundred and sixty-seven thin white sheep had jumped through the gap in the honeysuckle before her mind finally blanked out, and sleep overcame her.

It was one thirty-three in the morning when Kristin at last fell asleep. Grey knew the precise time because he had been confronting the lighted dial of his alarm clock at two-minute intervals ever since she refused to make love with him. He turned onto his back, staring blindly at the ceiling. He could feel cold sweat beading on his forehead, and his entire body ached from the effort of lying still for two hours, feigning indifference to the soft enticement of Kristin's body. He had been deeply hurt by her obvious lack of trust when she rejected his love-making so fiercely. Now he wondered with a touch of cynicism why he had allowed his pride to interfere so disastrously with his other needs and emotions. Unfulfilled sexual desire made a lousy nightcap.

He clasped his hands behind his head, suspecting that sleep was once again likely to prove impossible, and worrying because he needed to rest in order to get his body into top-notch condition. He was going to require all his reserves of strength before the next couple of weeks were over, and there had been too many sleepless nights recently.

He felt the familiar twist of tension curl in the pit of his stomach, clawing tight at his gut. His explanations to Kris had been feeble, he knew, but he had never before needed to lie to somebody he loved so much, and his usual skill at improvisation had completely deserted him. He wondered if, at some deeply buried level of his subconscious, he was hoping Kris would find out the truth. Maybe that's why his stories had been so inadequate.

On the other hand, if she loved him—really loved him in the way he loved her—wouldn't she accept his word, however unlikely it seemed? Wouldn't she understand that he could never lie about his feelings for her or his faithfulness to their marriage vows?

The questions remained as painful and as unanswerable as they had been two hours earlier. He knew only that his need for Kris's lovemaking had left a wrenching pain in his loins, and his need to confide in her had left a pounding ache in his heart.

He rolled over once again and glanced involuntarily at the clock. One-forty. Screw them all, he thought, clenching his fists into tight balls in the intensity of his frustration. He could carry obedience to regulations only so far. He was going to tell Kristin the truth before he left for Austria, and be damned to Steve Callahan and all the rest of the bureaucrats in Washington.

Chapter Seven

THE ALARM WENT off punctually at six-thirty the following morning. Kristin reached out groggily and pressed
the button, snuggling deeper under the covers. After less
than five hours' sleep she didn't exactly feel ready to
spring out of bed and greet the morning with a song.

When she finally stumbled into the bathroom, she
realized that Grey was not only up but apparently showered and dressed as well. As she brushed her teeth, she
could hear the murmur of voices in the kitchen, and the
smell of freshly brewed coffee drifted in through the
bedroom door.

She slammed into the shower, her anger simmering
as the spray poured over her. No wonder Grey was up
and about so early! The wretched man had been sleeping
peacefully since eleven o'clock the night before. Whereas
she... She allowed the thought to trail away as she

dressed in a clean white uniform, brushing her hair into a loose knot at the nape of her neck and putting on her makeup. She applied an extra layer of foundation under her eyes, hoping to conceal the shadows caused by her restless night. When she was done, she squinted into the mirror. She certainly looked a whole lot fresher than she felt, even under the brightness of a fluorescent light. How lucky women were that society allowed them to disguise their faces with makeup. Men had a tougher time of it in that respect.

Steve Callahan jumped courteously to his feet when she entered the kitchen. Grey had his back toward her, preparing a grapefruit at the kitchen counter, and she noticed that he didn't immediately turn around.

"Good morning," she said to Steve with forced cheerfulness. "That coffee smells wonderful. I hope you slept well?"

"Beautifully, thanks. Your spare bed's very comfortable. And there was no baby around to demand her two-o'clock feeding, which was definitely a plus."

Kristin produced another polite smile, swallowing over the angry lump in her throat. This man was a liar, she reminded herself, and she wasn't going to let herself like him, however pleasant he managed to appear. She poured herself a mug of black coffee and put some whole wheat bread into the toaster, avoiding Steve's gaze.

"You're up early, Grey," she said with a sweet smile. "I hope you slept well, too." She leaned against the sink as she sipped her coffee, feeling pleased with the apparent casualness of her tone.

"Yes, I slept well, but I have to make an early start. We have a couple of important meetings scheduled at the university this morning. I need to leave within fifteen minutes."

Grey finally turned around as he finished speaking, and she was shocked by the weariness she saw etched deep into his features. Tight lines of strain stretched from his nose to his mouth, giving him an uncharacteristically grim expression. If she hadn't known better, she would have said he looked like somebody who had spent the entire night without sleep.

She hardened her heart. It was time to find out what Grey was hiding from her. It was not the time to feel sorry for him because he looked so exhausted.

"Do you have your suitcase already packed?" she asked with a false appearance of solicitude. "I put a stack of clean shirts in your dresser drawer yesterday."

"Yes, thanks. Everything's ready." He took a couple of spoonfuls of grapefruit, then got up from the table and pushed the almost untouched fruit into the garbage disposal. "Kristin... about this trip of mine..."

"If you two will excuse me, I'll leave you to make your plans." Steve Callahan rose to his feet and carried his empty coffee mug over to the kitchen sink. "I guess Kristin still needs to hear some details about your stay in Philadelphia."

"I've already explained that my schedule is a little indefinite," Grey said with a curious lack of emphasis.

"It's tough when these open-ended business trips come up," Steve agreed. "It's irritating not knowing when somebody's going to get home."

For some reason Grey's voice hardened with an edge of irony. "You needn't worry about a thing, Steve. I've made all the appropriate excuses to my wife."

A sudden silence descended on the kitchen, and it seemed to Kristin that it was a silence fraught with tension. It was Steve Callahan who spoke first. "Well, I still have to clear my shaving things out of the guest bathroom, so thanks again, Kristin, for your hospitality. It was a terrific dinner, and it was great not to have to spend the night in a hotel. I travel so much I get sick of hotel rooms." He looked across the kitchen toward Grey, his expression unreadable. "I'll be ready to leave whenever you say. Just give me a shout."

"We've enjoyed having you here," Kristin replied mechanically. She thought how astonishing it was that the rules governing civilized behavior were so deeply ingrained that it was almost impossible to say what she really felt. "Thank you for the gift. Please come and visit us again when business brings you to Denver."

Steve nodded his acknowledgment as he left the kitchen, and Kristin busied herself with spreading butter and honey on her toast. Out of the corner of her eye she saw Grey run his hand through his hair, then knead the muscles at the back of his neck in an unconscious betrayal of tiredness.

"Grey, are you feeling all right?" The soft question escaped before she remembered how mad at him she was.

He straightened immediately, the impression of weariness vanishing behind an easygoing grin. "I'm feeling fine, honey. All I need is ten minutes in the gym to work out a few early-morning kinks. Ever since Steve complained about getting old, I've been feeling my joints creak. He used to be the campus daredevil, you know. I can't quite get used to picturing him changing diapers."

Kristin found she was no longer deceived by Grey's flippant manner. As if blinkers had been removed from her eyes, she realized how much effort had gone into giving that seemingly easy response. She suddenly saw the tension lurking behind his casual stance at the counter, the strain lingering behind his offhand manner.

With some difficulty she squashed a last trace of sympathy for him. She was sick to death of being humored as if she were a brainless child. She wanted some straight answers for once and she wanted them now.

"Are you coming home for dinner tonight?" she asked brusquely.

"No. I'm sorry. I thought I already explained that I'm catching an early-evening flight, and there's no time to come back to the apartment. I'd have to leave for the airport almost before we could sit down to eat."

"I see. Well, in that case it certainly isn't worth coming home."

A plan of action had been percolating in her subconscious during the night, and now it bubbled to the surface. She didn't want to provide Grey with an opportunity to frustrate her scheme, so she needed to avoid any discussion until it was too late for him to stop her. She would call his office during the day, she decided, and set the wheels in motion. Direct confrontation with Grey had gotten her nowhere, so she would obviously have to try a more subtle approach if she wanted to discover what was going on. It was time for her to be crafty rather than accusatory.

She finished her last bite of toast and smiled brightly at Grey, stashed her plate in the dishwasher, and rinsed honey from her fingers under the kitchen tap. "Well, I'm sorry we won't be seeing one another for a while, but I have to run now. My first patient is expecting me in exactly twenty-five minutes, so I'd better start praying there are no holdups on the highway."

Grey seemed startled by her cheeriness. "I'll call you tomorrow from Philadelphia," he said. "I should have a better idea of my schedule by then."

"Great," she said. He moved toward her with the obvious intention of giving her a long and sensuous kiss, but she slipped to one side and put the honey back in the cupboard. She blew a kiss into the air somewhere near his cheek, just as if she hadn't realized he hoped for a far more passionate farewell. She evaded his outstretched arm and made a dash for the hall closet, pulling out the first jacket her hand touched. Fortunately it was one of her own.

"See you soon, Grey," she called. "Have a good trip. Tell the pilot to drive carefully." Within thirty seconds she was out of the apartment. To her relief, nobody followed.

She called Grey's office during her lunch break. As she had expected, Sue answered the phone.

"Hello, Sue." Kristin was careful to keep her voice

at its most sunny and ingenuous. Her jaws were beginning to ache with the strain of producing so many artificial smiles. "May I have a word with Grey, please?"

"He's in a departmental meeting right at the moment, Kristin."

"Could you get him out? I promise I'll only take five minutes of his time. I have some good news for him."

"I'll see what I can do."

Now that her suspicions were alerted, Kristin thought she could hear a distinct trace of hesitation in the secretary's voice, and she wondered precisely what was causing it. What could possibly be threatening about a wife asking to speak to her husband for a few minutes?

"Hold on for a moment, please," Sue added.

Grey sounded unusually curt when he picked up the phone. "Yes, Kristin, what is it?"

She unconsciously crossed her fingers in a childish gesture to ward off the guilt caused by telling a lie. "Oh, Grey, I have some good news! My supervisor wants to test out a new physio, and the two of them are going to take my childbirth preparation class this afternoon. So I can get off work at three o'clock."

"Kristin, that's terrific, but I'm in the middle of an important meeting, and I have no time to talk. I'll phone you this evening from the airport."

"But that's the reason I'm calling now," Kristin said hurriedly. "I want us to have dinner together before you leave for Philadelphia." She lowered her voice to a husky plea. "I...I want to make up for what happened last night, Grey. Now that I have this unexpected time off, I can meet you at a restaurant near the airport, and there's no need for you to come home. What time would you like us to meet? And which restaurant? It's your choice."

He didn't reply immediately. She could almost hear the mental wheels turning as he analyzed the implications of her suggestion. "Well, dinner together does sound like a great idea," he said finally. "But it would have to be a quick meal, Kris. We'd better eat actually at the airport, because I won't have time for anything long and fancy."

"Anywhere's fine. How about the coffee shop between the concourses? The one next to United Airlines."

"Sounds fine. I'll be there at five o'clock."

As soon as she put down the phone, Kristin went to her supervisor's office. "Dorothy, I'm sorry to spring this on you, but I need an indefinite leave of absence from the hospital. I ought to be back within the week, but I can't promise. I wouldn't ask, but it's urgent."

Dorothy peered over her bifocals. "This is a heck of a day to ask for time off. We're short-staffed as it is, and you have a couple of patients who really need you."

Kristin flushed guiltily. "I know. I realize Missy Gordon doesn't respond well to strangers, and she's at an important stage in her treatment. But I'll go see her before I leave and try to explain why I have to go away. And I'll talk to her parents. I'll call Tom Mareno as well, just to make sure he goes to those rehabilitation classes. Dorothy, I feel terrible about this, but I have to go. I wouldn't ask unless it was very important."

"Family problems?" her supervisor asked. "Nobody's sick, I hope."

"No, not that. Grey . . . my husband has to go away for a while, and I have to go with him. It's really important for both of us, Dorothy. And the worst of it is that I need to leave this afternoon, by three at the latest."

"Who on earth is going to take your Lamaze class if you leave at three?"

Kristin removed a nonexistent piece of fluff from her uniform. "I . . . er . . . I thought you might do it, Dorothy. You know you have a soft spot for pregnant mothers."

"And who's going to fill out the six dozen urgent Medicaid forms on my desk if I'm off teaching a class this afternoon? Did you think of that when you were coming up with your great idea?"

"Dorothy, you know those government forms are practically self-regenerating. Let them wait for an afternoon; only the computer will know you've sinned."

Her supervisor hid a tiny smile. "What will you do if I refuse permission for a leave of absence?" she asked with an attempt at severity.

Kristin drew in a deep breath. "I'll take one anyway."

"I thought you might say that." The supervisor picked up a pen and twisted it around in her fingers before speaking. "All right, you have your leave of absence. But I'll expect you to volunteer for at least thirty hours of overtime when you get back."

"You have it," Kristin said. "It's a deal. Maybe even forty hours! Thanks, Dorothy."

"You'd better get out of here before I change my mind. And don't get pregnant while you're gone. My soft spot for pregnant mothers doesn't extend to members of my staff. Remember, you've got forty hours of overtime to fit in before I'll let you claim maternity leave."

Kristin's smile faded. "Don't worry, Dorothy. I can promise you pregnancy isn't in my plans right now."

She left the hospital before three and drove home along the same route she had followed the previous Friday. The sun shone every bit as brightly, and the mountains appeared just as spectacular against the blue horizon. This time, however, her mood was far different from her previous euphoria.

She packed her suitcase with a grim sense that the future of her marriage was quite possibly at stake. She had no idea where she was going or how long she was likely to be away, so it wasn't easy to choose suitable clothing. She did know, however, that when Grey got on his plane that evening, she was going to be with him. At least one other thing seemed fairly clear in her mind: If she found herself attending a series of meetings at the University of Pennsylvania, she'd be extremely surprised. She'd lay odds on the fact that, whatever Grey was planning to do, geology meetings didn't come into it.

She was too pressed for time to spend long debating

what to pack. In the end, she settled on a basic supply of underwear and a selection of medium-weight skirts, light blouses, and thick sweaters. Unless Grey was going to Florida or Alaska, she had the fall climate of the States pretty well provided for. She added her toiletries and a small bag of makeup to her luggage, but this time she didn't include any fancy black nightgowns. The state of her marriage seemed too precarious for that sort of frivolity.

She put on a gray wool dress and collected her coat from the hall closet. She wanted to be at the airport well before five o'clock so she could conceal her suitcase somewhere before Grey arrived.

Just as she was about to close the front door, she realized that she ought to clear out the refrigerator. She stepped back into the apartment and quickly emptied half a carton of milk down the sink. She threw out assorted leftovers and then disposed of the garbage. She made sure all the lights were turned off and dialed the thermostat to low. Finally, she checked her purse to see that she had a credit card to pay for her airline ticket. When she was confident everything was properly arranged, she left the apartment. As she headed for her car, she wondered where she would be sleeping that night.

She was sitting at a small corner table sipping iced water when Grey arrived at the coffee shop. He gave her a quick kiss before slipping into the chair opposite hers.

"Sorry I'm late. The meetings today went on forever." His eyes crinkled as he smiled at her, and she felt her stomach give a little lurch of love and longing. "Have you ordered?"

"No, although I've looked at the menu. The choice seems to be limited to plain hamburgers or hamburgers with fancy toppings. Unless you want a salad."

"Men only order salads when their wives are watching. You're not watching, are you, Kris?"

"Since I suggested we should eat together, I guess

not." She smiled. "Just for tonight you can eat unhealthy food with my blessing."

The waitress arrived to take their orders, and Kristin requested a shrimp cocktail and a fresh-fruit salad. She watched with mock horror as Grey ordered a cheese-burger topped with mushrooms, onions, green peppers, and bacon. He asked the waitress to bring him an extra-large serving of french fries. "And a big bottle of ketchup, please."

Kristin swallowed her laughter. "I gather you missed lunch?"

"Yes, actually I did." He patted his flat stomach, his eyes alight with mischief. "Eat your heart out, honey. And don't ask me for any french fries because I won't give you a single one."

"I don't like french fries. They're loaded with grease and calories and devoid of vitamins. They're potential heart attacks disguised as bite-sized morsels of food."

"That's what you always say, my sweet, but it never seems to stop you from sneaking them off my plate when you think I'm not looking."

She glared at him. "Have I ever mentioned that you're totally obnoxious when you're smug?"

He simply laughed. "Mmm...here comes my ham-burger. I can smell that bacon from here."

The food proved to be unusually good for an airport coffee shop, and they both ate with relish. Grey was a charming dinner companion. He had obviously decided that, since this was likely to be their only meal together for several days, no ripple of anger or dissension was to mar it.

Kristin responded appropriately to his banter and smiled when he teased her, but she felt as if thick veils had finally been removed from before her eyes, and she was seeing her husband for the first time. She looked past the superficial amiability and saw the complex emotions seething beneath the surface charm. She probed even more deeply and suddenly recognized the effort Grey was exerting to keep his emotions under such tight control. He was exhausted, she realized. He was worried about something. Yet he was determined that she have a pleasant evening.

For the first time she began to understand the intense, disciplined dynamism of her husband's character. How had she ever allowed his mask of easygoing nonchalance to deceive her?

When they had finished their coffee, Grey pushed back his chair. "Kris, I wish I didn't have to leave, but I'll miss my plane if I'm not careful." He came and stood beside her, bending down and twining his fingers into her hair as he kissed her good-bye. She trembled as she felt the yearning in the touch of his lips against her mouth. His hand hovered for a moment over her breast, then, as if he remembered suddenly where they were, he reluctantly withdrew from her embrace.

"I'll call you tomorrow, sweetheart, and let you know when I'll be back." His friendly words belied the longing she had felt in his kiss. "Take care, Kris, and promise me you'll be careful. No more nonsense about letting strangers into the apartment."

"All right, I promise." Kristin walked with him toward the cashier's desk. "But I do still have a question for you, Grey."

"Yes?"

"Are you flying direct to Philadelphia, or are you making a diversion? Via Washington, maybe?"

He drew in a sharp, angry breath. "Kris, for heaven's sake don't start that argument again, not right now. We've been over it too many times already. Will you please put all your weird ideas about Washington and mistresses out of your mind?"

"You've done it again, haven't you, Grey?"

"Done what?" he asked. He took her hand and pulled her out of the cashier's line, pushing her in front of him until they were in a relatively secluded corner of the lobby. "Look, Kris, we've had a pleasant meal together.

Can't we end the evening without an argument?"

She ignored his plea. "You evaded my question, Grey. You avoided telling me a lie by the simple method of not answering the question I asked you."

"Dammit, I've already forgotten the question you asked!"

"Then I'll ask it again," she said tersely. "Are you flying direct to Philadelphia?"

"Yes, yes, yes! Yes, I'm flying direct to Philadelphia!"

She looked him straight in the eye. "How are you flying? By balloon or carrier pigeon? The last scheduled flight for Philadelphia left here at four fifty-four. I took the precaution of checking the flight schedules before I left home this evening. It's now six o'clock, so if you're flying to Philadelphia, I'd like to know how and on what."

Grey muttered a long, fluent, and highly inventive stream of profanities. He ran his hand through his hair and grabbed her by the wrist.

"Okay, Kristin, you want mystery and adventure? You want cloak-and-dagger stuff? Guess what, baby, you've got it!"

He marched out of the restaurant, dragging her along behind him.

"Grey," Kristin murmured, "you haven't paid the check!"

He swung around, fished in his pocket for a couple of bills, and dumped them down by the cash register. Not waiting for the change, he swung around again and stormed out of the coffee shop, his hand still firmly clamped around Kristin's wrist.

"My—my suitcase," she said. She had to run to keep up with his long strides, and she was tottering on her high heels. She felt utterly ridiculous. "Grey, my suitcase is in one of those lockers over there."

He stopped short in his purposeful march and turned

to stare at her. "You brought a suitcase? You planned on coming with me?"

She gulped, feeling her cheeks flame. "Yes."

"Well, that's just great, Kristin, because I sure as hell am planning on taking you. Let's get your suitcase."

They retrieved her luggage in silence, and Grey resumed his previous rapid march across the concourse. He now held Kristin's suitcase in one hand and her wrist in the other. She continued to trot along at his side.

"Grey, where are we going?"

"To the plane. You'll probably be astonished to hear that I rarely travel by balloon, and I've never traveled by carrier pigeon."

They walked to the far end of the terminal, then, when it seemed as if there was nowhere left for them to go except through a concrete wall, Grey stopped in front of an unobtrusive steel door, painted the same neutral color as the wall. *No Admittance* was marked on it in small but clear letters. Grey rapped twice, and the door opened at once to reveal a guard dressed in some sort of olive-drab uniform that Kristin didn't recognize. Grey displayed a small plastic identification card, and the guard saluted smartly.

"Evening, sir. Your plane has arrived. It's waiting for you."

"Thank you. Is there transportation to get me to the plane, or can we walk it?"

"No, sir. It's on the far runway. There's a Jeep outside."

Grey didn't need to warn Kristin to keep quiet. She couldn't have spoken if her life had depended on it. She was so stunned that she felt sure she must look less than half-witted. She tried to smile at the guard as she walked past, but her facial muscles, along with the rest of her body, seemed to be shocked into near-catatonic numbness. The guard escorted them down a narrow, unpainted corridor until they reached yet another steel door. This one opened electronically, apparently in response to some signal from the guard. A rush of wind greeted them as the door swung open, and they emerged into the coolness of the night.

A Jeep, with a young man already seated behind the wheel, waited for their arrival. Grey displayed his identification for the second time, and the young man opened the door for them to climb in.

It took about five minutes to reach their destination, which, as far as Kristin could tell, was simply a deserted corner of Stapleton Airport. A small plane stood at the end of a lighted runway. There was only one runway in the vicinity and only one plane. In the distance, Kristin could hear the roar of jet engines as planes took off and landed at regular intervals.

"We've arrived," Grey said to her, his voice unexpectedly gentle after his flare of temper. When she didn't move, he reached back into the Jeep, lifted her out, and set her on the ground. As soon as she was out of the car, the driver saluted and drove away.

A figure appeared in the lighted doorway of the aircraft, and, with a sensation of absolute inevitability, Kristin recognized the blond hair and powerful build of Steve Callahan.

"Hello, Grey. You're ten minutes late." There was a note of laughter threading through Callahan's voice. "Did you run into a spot of difficulty?"

"You could say that." There was no answering humor in Grey's reply. "I've brought my wife with me," he said. "She's coming with us. I'm taking her to meet Smith."

"What an unexpected pleasure for Mr. Smith." This time there was no mistaking the amusement in Steve's gaze as he looked at them both. "Since we don't have a stewardess, I guess I'd better do the honors. Welcome aboard, Kristin. I hope you enjoy the flight."

"Where are we going?" She forced the words out

through lips that felt drier than desert sand.

It was Grey who answered her.

"To Washington," he said. "For an interview with my boss."

Chapter Eight

As soon as she climbed up the wobbly steel staircase and entered the small jet, Kristin saw that the pilot was wearing a military uniform, although she was too inexperienced to recognize the branch of the military from which he came. He was waiting in the cabin to greet Grey, standing just behind Steve Callahan, but his expression changed from courtesy to wariness when he saw that Grey hadn't boarded the plane alone. He removed his earphones, leaving them looped around his neck.

"Welcome aboard, sir," he said to Grey. The pilot glanced only once at Kristin, then stared into the middle distance, managing to look through her as effectively as if she hadn't been there.

"I have instructions for the transportation of only two passengers, sir. For security reasons, my orders are quite specific." His voice, though courteous, left no doubt that he not only was quite clear about his orders but also intended to follow them precisely.

"I'll sign fresh ones," Grey said curtly.

"But I'm afraid, sir, that would require somebody with the rank of—"

"I have the necessary authority." Grey's words were clipped. He pulled the identification that he had shown the Jeep driver from his pocket, and the pilot looked carefully at the small, laminated card.

He handed it back to Grey with evident respect. "Yes, indeed, sir, you sure do have the authority. I'll draw up the flight orders right away, and then we can notify the tower that we're ready for takeoff."

The pilot was unable to resist a second curious glance in Kristin's direction as he leaned across her to close the heavy door of the plane. She tried to smile casually, as if she knew exactly what she was doing on board a military jet and was confident she had every right to be there, but she was quite sure she looked as nervous and guilty as she felt. She leaned against the wall of the aircraft, unconsciously seeking the reassurance of something solid beneath her hands.

Steve had watched the entire exchange in silence. He didn't speak until the pilot replaced his earphones and returned to the cockpit.

"Pulling rank, Grey?" he asked then, a faint smile tugging at the edges of his mouth. "That's the first time I've ever seen you do it."

"Smith is going to tie my ass in a sling anyway. An altered manifest is likely to be the least of my worries tomorrow morning."

"That's probably true." Steve took a seat and strapped on his seat belt. "I have vivid memories of my own session with good old Mr. Smith, when I told him I was going back to England to marry Megan." He smiled faintly. "In case you don't know it, I should warn you that underneath Mr. Smith's gruff exterior beats a heart of solid, reinforced concrete."

"I'm well aware of Smith's views on family involvement in agency business," Grey said tersely. He looked at Kristin, his expression grim. "You'd better come and sit down," he said. "We're late, and I'm sure the pilot will want to make up lost time, if he can."

Kristin levered herself away from the wall and into the seat next to Grey's. Her hands were shaking so badly that she couldn't fasten her safety belt. Grey leaned over, his movements impatient as he clicked the latch into position. Except for the brief moment of gentleness when he lifted her from the Jeep, he had seemed furious with her from the time they'd left the restaurant.

The pilot returned with a clipboard and a sheaf of forms. Grey scrawled his signature at the foot of five different pages, and Kristin felt a spark of genuine amusement as she saw the multiple layers of carbon paper. How incredible it was, she thought, that even the most secret branches of the government apparently couldn't operate without forms filled out in triplicate.

"We have a four-hour flight plan," the pilot said. "We should be landing at 0125 Eastern time."

"Sounds good. We're ready to take off whenever you have permission."

The pilot left the cabin, closing the cockpit door behind him. Almost immediately, the plane taxied into position on the runway, and within minutes they were airborne. A sign flashed overhead indicating that they could unfasten their seat belts and smoke if they wished. Kristin felt another twist of amusement. It seemed incongruous to her that a plane designed for flying secret government missions should flash its message in such a routine fashion.

Steve Callahan got up from his seat. "I think, Grey, that it's time we had a little chat," he said.

Grey's mouth tightened into an even more forbidding

line. "Yes," he said. "I'll try to explain what happened."

He stood up. "Please stay in your seat, Kristin, unless you need to go to the washroom. I think you'll find a selection of current newsmagazines in the rack to your left."

Grey's words were polite, but he clearly was offering her no choice in the matter, and, without waiting for her to reply, he walked down the narrow aisle and joined Steve in the small lounge at the rear of the aircraft. They stayed there for most of the flight. Their voices remained low, but Kristin wasn't deceived. Just because they weren't shouting, it didn't mean that their discussion was harmonious. Even though her seat was some distance away, she could feel the angry intensity of their exchange. Steve Callahan didn't strike her as the type of man who would pay an exorbitant amount of attention to rules and regulations, so she wondered just what he and Grey were arguing about. It was distressing to conclude that she was very likely the cause of dissension between two men who were, presumably, friends as well as colleagues.

About half an hour before the plane landed, the two men returned to their seats. Steve pulled a copy of *National Geographic* magazine from his briefcase and soon seemed immersed in its contents. Grey turned stiffly toward Kristin, his eyes opaque and his expression completely inscrutable.

"I have Steve's permission to tell you that I'm currently engaged on a special assignment for the government."

"Is that all?"

"It's all that it's appropriate for me to tell you at this time."

Kristin's guilt at having forced Grey into a difficult position withered under the force of his coldness. Dammit, she was his wife! And he had lied to her, not once but dozens of times. Even now it seemed that he wasn't prepared to tell her anything meaningful.

"You sound like a government press release when they're trying to cover up something unforgivable," she said tightly. "Believe it or not, I'd worked out all by myself that you were doing something secret for the government. I may be a bit slow on the uptake, but I'm not a complete fool, despite what you and your colleagues in Washington seem to think."

"Nobody thinks you're a fool, Kristin. It's agency policy not to tell *anybody* anything they don't need to know."

"Don't need to know!" she exclaimed. "I'm your *wife*, Grey. I think that automatically means I have some right to know what you've been doing."

"Perhaps. Sometimes the decision isn't as simple as we'd like it to be. There are other people—other interests—involved in this situation."

"You don't trust me to keep quiet, is that it?" She covered her hurt with sarcasm. "Grey, even if I wanted to give away your secrets, I don't understand enough about shale-oil production to be any danger to anybody. You could give me the whole formula for whatever brilliant discovery you've made, and you know darn well I'd forget it within ten seconds."

He was silent for a long, tense moment. "I'm not working with the government on a scientific project," he said finally.

A quiver of fear rippled over her, settling into a hard knot somewhere near the bottom of her stomach. "Just what are you doing, Grey? If you're not involved in research work, what kind of *special assignment* could give you the right to fly in military planes and have passes that open locked doors at the airport? You're a mining engineer, Grey. What does the government want with you if it isn't scientific research?"

"I started work for the government as soon as I left college. I've had several years of...specialized ...training."

Questions took shape in her brain, but they seemed

to stick there, not emerging coherently from her throat. "What sort of . . . What do you mean, Grey? What kind of specialized training?"

A sudden thought struck her, and for some reason it added yet another weight to the burden of fear she carried. "What does that woman you were with last Friday— Narina somebody-or-other—what does she have to do with all this?"

The lines of weariness etched between Grey's nose and mouth seemed to deepen fractionally. His reply emerged in a harsh monotone, and Kristin was too over-wrought to hear the pain behind the flatness.

"I don't have permission to answer those questions," he said.

"Permission? Permission from whom? From Steve Callahan? Is he your boss or something?"

"No, not exactly. He's my liaison with headquarters, my control. I'm considered a field operative."

She gulped. "You're telling me that you work for the CIA, aren't you? What does . . . what does being a field operative mean?"

Steve Callahan's attention obviously was not as firmly rooted in the magazine as it had seemed. He looked toward them, his brilliant blue gaze unwillingly sympathetic. "Grey," he said quietly, "I'd leave any further explanations until tomorrow if I were you."

Anger flared briefly in Grey's eyes. "You've already made your views on this perfectly clear to me, Steve. On more than one occasion."

"I haven't necessarily made my views clear to you," Steve said with deliberate mildness. "I've occasionally reminded you of the agency's regulations."

At that moment the pilot came out of the cockpit. "I'm in touch with ground control; we'll be landing shortly. You'll be pleased to hear that we're almost on schedule."

For the first time in several hours Kristin forgot about the mysteries of Grey's occupation. Flying had never been one of her favorite pastimes, and she felt even less safe in this small jet than she did in the large commercial planes she was accustomed to. If she hadn't been in such a turmoil when the plane took off, she'd have been biting her nails. Since there was only one pilot on the plane, it made her extremely nervous to see him out of the flight seat.

"Er...I don't mean to sound rude, but shouldn't you get back to the controls?" she asked the pilot, trying to sound casual. "I wouldn't mention it, but since there isn't a copilot or a navigator or anything..."

"These jets are designed to be flown by a single pilot, ma'am."

She wasn't reassured. "I always thought it needed the captain's steady hand on the joystick when a plane came in to land."

The pilot's stern features relaxed into a genuine smile. "This plane doesn't have a joystick, ma'am. Actually, it's on automatic pilot at the moment, and the computer could probably land the plane quite safely even if I passed out or something."

Kristin swallowed hard. "What happens if the computer malfunctions?"

Steve Callahan and the pilot exchanged infuriatingly condescending grins. "There's a backup system," Steve explained. "But, as it happens, both Grey and I could fly this plane if we had to. So you actually have three pilots on board."

Kristin looked at her husband in mute disbelief. He returned her look with a cool glance tinged with a hint of mockery.

"You can fly?" she croaked.

He nodded. Somehow the simple fact that Grey could fly a jet seemed more extraordinary than anything else she had learned that evening. Perhaps it was merely that her mind could just about grasp the strangeness of this fact, whereas the other revelations seemed so absurd, so outrageous, that the rational part of her brain still refused to accept them.

The pilot returned to his seat, clicking into his harness but leaving the cockpit door open. His conversation with the control tower was inaudible, but it seemed to Kristin that he flicked buttons with a bone-chilling degree of casualness.

There was no opportunity to press Grey for any further details of his work with the CIA. The plane touched down smoothly and taxied a short distance along the runway. The door swung open, and the familiar steel steps were wheeled out for their descent. Once Steve and Grey had displayed their passes, the three of them were allowed to exit the plane and proceed unescorted to the terminal building. They had landed at Andrews Air Force Base, Kristin realized, and not at one of Washington's regular civilian airports. It was one-thirty in the morning, but the base seemed very busy with planes taking off at regular intervals and a fair number of people hurrying through the terminal.

Steve's own Buick was, so he said, waiting for him in a nearby parking lot. A government car was supposed to be waiting for Grey outside the terminal, but it wasn't in its assigned spot.

"Wait here with Steve," Grey said to Kristin, a hint of weariness in his voice. "I'll go and sort things out."

He walked over to a desk at the far corner of the terminal, and Steve's gaze followed his progress for a minute before he turned to look consideringly at Kristin. "Be kind to him tonight," he said softly. "Grey's had a lousy couple of months."

She stiffened, resenting the implication that it was her responsibility to soothe Grey's ruffled feelings, resenting even more the fact that Steve obviously considered her likely to be unsympathetic.

Her voice tightened with an involuntary surge of hostility. "It hasn't exactly been peachy-dreamy for me these past few weeks, you know. It's not only Grey who's been suffering."

"Grey's been struggling to reconcile two conflicting obligations," Steve said quietly. "That's a hell of a strain for any man, and it's especially hard for Grey. He has a strong sense of duty combined with an acute sensitivity to other people's feelings. He knows exactly what he's been doing to you, and he hates himself for it. He understands what it was like for you when you were growing up, Kristin, and he knows how badly you want security and a steady home life. On top of all that, the guy is head over heels in love with you and not absolutely certain that you return his love. That's a pretty lethal combination. And in Grey's line of work, with the assignment he has ahead of him, it could be literally lethal if you don't ease up on the guy."

Her eyes widened with terror. "What do you mean?"

Steve's expression immediately became closed once more. "Grey has maintained all along that you're a strong, understanding woman, Kristin. Don't let him down. Right now he needs your love and loyalty very badly."

Before she could ask anything more, Grey had joined them. "Our car's finally ready," he said. He looked at Kristin and then at Steve. "What have you been telling her?" he asked brusquely.

Steve gave Grey a friendly punch on the arm. "Nothing much. Kristin was saying how much she's looking forward to tomorrow's meeting with Mr. Smith."

Grey grunted. "Ignorance is certainly bliss. If she'd ever met the man, she'd know better."

Steve laughed, withdrawing a set of car keys from his pocket. "Well, I'm off home. I've no doubt there'll be a note on the kitchen table telling me that, since I'm so late anyway, it's my turn to feed Stephanie." He gave an exaggerated sigh. "You'd think modern medical science would have come up with some way to convince babies to sleep through the night."

A trace of a smile softened Grey's harsh expression. "If you didn't have the excuse of feeding her, you'd wake her up anyway."

Steve's eyes crinkled at the corners. "Maybe you're right."

He touched Kristin lightly on the arm. "I've enjoyed meeting you," he said. "I look forward to seeing you again."

Grey was already directing Kristin's steps toward the car. "I'll be in touch with you tomorrow, Steve."

Less than fifteen minutes later, Grey turned the car into the parking lot of a secluded hotel in a quiet section of Washington. Kristin followed him into the deserted lobby, hardly blinking when she saw him sign their names at the reception desk as Mr. and Mrs. Paul Mason. She did swallow rather hard when she saw him produce a driver's license that supposedly confirmed his identity as Paul Mason. It was the little things, she thought, the trivial reminders of deception, that were so difficult to accept. Their flight from Denver on a government jet somehow seemed less extraordinary than the fact that Grey possessed a forged official document from the state of Maryland.

The receptionist apologized for the absence of a bell-boy and handed them their room key. "It's on the third floor, to the right as you come out of the elevator."

It was a pleasant enough room, decorated in typical hotel shades of beige, cream, and brown. Kristin put her small suitcase on the bed and turned to face Grey, feeling a peculiar, nervous fluttering in her stomach. She realized, to her astonishment, that on top of all her other churned-up emotions, she was feeling shy. She felt as if she'd walked into the hotel room with a stranger, and, looking at Grey's dark, unreadable features, she understood why. At this moment Grey *was* a stranger to her. He scarcely even looked like the man she thought she knew. He was moving quickly between the closet, the bathroom, and the bed, unpacking his suitcase. His expression was forbidding. His actions were crisp, sharp, efficient. Even the way he walked seemed unfamiliar.

She cleared her throat. "Grey, we have to talk. You have to tell me what this is all about. I . . . I feel as if I don't know you. I feel like I'm married to a virtual stranger."

"I'm sorry about that," he said. "But tonight isn't the right time for explanations. It's late. I'm tired, and I have a hell of a lot more on my mind than the need to give you self-serving justifications for what I've done."

"Don't you think I'm entitled—"

"I don't think anything. Right now I'm not in the mood for thinking. I'm too exhausted to think." He walked around the bed and closed his hands around her arms, drawing her forcefully against his body. "I've spent too many nights recently lying awake, wanting you. I don't plan to spend tonight the same way. We're not going to talk; we're going to make love."

"I don't appreciate being *told* that, Grey. Making love is supposed to be—"

"Shut up, Kristin," he said softly, and his mouth came down to take hers in a burning, mind-destroying kiss.

She resisted at first, startled by the urgency of his lips as they moved roughly against her mouth. His hands ran slowly over her breasts and hips, their stroking passionate and unrestrained.

Slowly, unwillingly, she felt her lips part, felt herself accept the hard thrust of his tongue into her mouth. Her breath became uneven, and her hands moved up restlessly to bury themselves in his thick, dark hair.

As soon as he recognized her compliance, he curved his hand more tightly around her bottom, pulling her hard against him, thrusting his knee between her legs. With a jolt of surprise, she realized that tonight Grey was intent upon conquering her body. He didn't intend to persuade her into cooperation; he wanted the satisfaction of overcoming her resistance.

A strange excitement twisted along her veins, and a flush of heat rushed beneath her skin. Her mind still throbbed with a hundred questions, but her body didn't care whether or not Grey gave any answers. She felt an unfamiliar mingling of tenderness, passion, and bewilderment as Grey's hands ruthlessly explored her body. But most of all, she soon realized, she felt acute, burning desire. She trembled in his arms, and her head arched back instinctively as he dropped a line of brief, hard kisses along the soft curve of her jaw.

Grey lifted his head from her throat, and she saw the dark glitter of his eyes. "Take off your clothes, Kristin," he ordered quietly. There was no gentleness in his command, only dominance, demand, and the throb of sexual urgency.

Her hands went obediently to the zipper of her dress before she registered exactly what she was doing, and then she felt a ripple of something close to fear snake down her spine. She jerked herself out of his embrace, whirling around to conceal the desire she knew still lingered in her eyes.

Her thoughts were chaotic. He had almost succeeded in making her lose control, something she had always sworn she would never do. She didn't want to submit to Grey while she was in the throes of this helpless yearning for sexual fulfillment. She loved Grey, she admired him, but she didn't want to surrender completely to him. She never wanted to surrender herself completely to any man. Living with her egocentric parents had taught her the art of self-protection at a very young age. She knew all too well what rejected love felt like, and she had always realized that she needed to keep some tiny part of herself in reserve. In her relationship with Grey, even during their most passionate lovemaking, there had always been some fraction of herself that she held back as protection against the fear of his rejection. And the discoveries she had made recently about Grey made it more important than ever that she should retain some protective barriers around her heart. She needed to cling to the control her mind had always exercised over her body.

Her hands fell to her sides, and she struggled to hide the note of desire that roughened her voice when she finally turned around to face him. "Cavemen may have told their mates to take off their leopard skins, Grey, but I don't appreciate being ordered around. Our marriage is supposed to be an equal partnership. You ought to know I'm not turned on by the slave-girl-and-her-master routine."

His eyes gleamed darkly, and his brows rose a notch, giving his features an arrogant cast she had never seen before. "Get your clothes off, Kristin, or I'll have the greatest pleasure ripping them off." For a fleeting instant the tight line of his mouth softened into a smile. "If you want equal rights, I'll promise to take my clothes off, too."

She glared at him in breathless defiance. "I'm not getting undressed at your command," she said. "I'm not planning to make love tonight."

Even while she spoke, she had a flash of unwelcome insight into her own motives. Her mind had defied him because she resented the implications of his command, but her body had defied him because she wanted him to overcome her resistance. Her body was signaling to both of them that she wanted him to throw her on the bed and make love to her until she had no individual will, no mind of her own.

She twisted away from Grey, panicked by her new perception of herself. He caught her easily, pulling down the zipper of her dress and stripping the garment from her body. In a few controlled, relentless movements, he ripped off the rest of her clothing. He pushed her suitcase off the bed with a single sweep of his arm, then picked her up and tossed her on top of the covers.

She started to fight him, while deep inside her soul she carried the sickening realization that she only fought him in the hope that he would force her to surrender. He straddled her body, capturing her thighs between his legs, and within seconds she was flat on her back, her hands pinned uselessly above her head. Still holding her immobile, his mouth closed over her breast, and she arched against him in a shuddering, humiliating betrayal of her need.

"Do you want me to make love to you now?" he asked huskily.

"No!" Pride forced the denial from her. His hands moved softly against her, and the quiver of her body revealed her lie.

"I love you, Kristin. There's no need to be afraid."

She didn't want to think about how much that statement revealed. She didn't want Grey to understand her too completely. Her body twisted helplessly against his, and with some distant part of her consciousness she accepted that she no longer struggled in defiance but rather in a desperate plea for fulfillment. The rough wool of Grey's trousers rubbed against her naked thigh, and she realized suddenly that he was still almost fully clothed. With a wrenching jolt of despair, she realized something more important. Despite his own urgent state of arousal, Grey wasn't going to complete their union until she admitted how much she wanted him. Tonight, as he had never done before, he was going to make her voice her terrifying dependence on him.

"Do you want me to make love to you now?" he asked again. His mouth toyed with her breasts; his fingers stroked her to the brink of ecstasy and then stopped, tantalizing her, frustrating her almost beyond endurance.

She didn't want to admit how desperately she needed him, despite the way her body craved release. She struggled to hold on to that tiny corner of her soul that had so far kept her free of total dependence on Grey. Confused and overwrought, she felt tears gather at the corners of her eyes and roll slowly down her cheeks.

Immediately Grey's hands were gentle against her skin, cupping her face as he kissed her long and deep.

His thumbs brushed away the tears. "I love you, Kristin," he said quietly. "I love you more than anybody or anything in the world."

When he spoke, she no longer remembered why she was fighting him. Certainly she no longer cared. She reached out, tugging at the buttons of his shirt, frantic in the urgency of her need for him.

"Make love to me," she said. "Grey, please don't make me wait any longer."

It was only a few seconds before his clothes followed hers into an untidy heap on the floor, but to Kristin it seemed a lifetime. When he was undressed he took her in his arms, cradling her against the warmth of his chest. Her mouth parted with aching hunger beneath his, and her hips writhed upward to receive him. She moved insistently against him, but he held her hips still, forcing her to delay the moment of climax. He kissed her again, murmuring incoherent words of love against her skin until she could no longer feel where her flesh ended and his body began. When he finally took her, she was overwhelmed by the violence of her own reaction, shuddering with ecstasy in the hard, hot circle of his arms.

He kissed her lingeringly as they came down from the heights, then he threw back the covers, and they slipped together between the sheets. He said nothing to her as he leaned over and gave her a final quick, hard kiss. Within less than a minute, he had fallen asleep.

Kristin turned off the bedside lamp and lay staring into the darkness. Her body ached with the afterglow of a fulfillment more complete than any she had ever known, while her heart ached with a burden of new self-knowledge. She knew that tonight a watershed in her marriage had been reached and traversed. Tonight, finally, Grey had forced her to acknowledge openly what she had always secretly known: She loved him with an intensity and a depth that recognized no limits. However badly she might want to protect herself from the pain of loving a man too much, tonight Grey had proven to her that her wants were pointless. Her happiness was within his keeping, and she had no power to protect herself from any pain he might inflict on her.

It was only as she was drifting into sleep that another thought occurred to her. It was true that Grey possessed the power to hurt her, but he had deliberately avoided using it. Tonight, at the end, when they both knew he could have taken her with the most humiliating display of macho aggression, he had held her in his arms and told her that he loved her.

She turned on her side so that she could look at Grey and saw that, for once, he looked young and totally relaxed while he slept. Unable to prevent herself, she reached out to stroke the tanned breadth of his shoulders.

Now, when it was safe, when he couldn't hear the words and use them against her, she whispered the truth. "I love you, Grey. I love you so much that it hurts."

As she had known there would be, there was only silence from the other side of the bed.

Chapter Nine

KRISTIN AGREED WITH Grey that they shouldn't go into the hotel restaurant for breakfast. They ordered coffee and sweet rolls from room service and ate in a polite and somewhat wary silence. When Kristin began to pick up her clothes from the floor, shaking the crumpled gray dress before laying it in her suitcase, Grey finally spoke. "I'm sorry about last night."

"There's no reason to be sorry."

"I was afraid I might have—hurt you." He glanced into the mirror, seemingly preoccupied with the knot of his tie. "You asked me once if I ever lost my temper. Well, I lost it last night, and you saw what happened."

"I found it rather... exciting."

Kristin felt the heat flame fiercely in her cheeks as he swung around to look at her. A tiny grin suddenly quirked his mouth.

"The old slave-girl-and-her-master routine has some appeal after all? I'm amazed at you, Kris."

She felt her flush deepen, but she didn't pursue the subject. "What's going to happen this morning, Grey? How do you know your boss will agree to see me?"

"Steve Callahan undoubtedly notified him last night about the breach of security." Grey's voice became dry. "If Smith hadn't wanted to see you, somebody from the agency would have arrived by now to escort you back to Denver."

"Are you sure he'll agree that you can tell me what's going on?"

"I'll make sure that he agrees," Grey said grimly.

It was still early when they checked out of the hotel— paying their bill with a Paul Mason credit card, Kristin noticed—and drove to a crowded side street in the center of Washington. She had expected Grey to take her to the official CIA headquarters. Instead, he parked the car in the underground garage of a somewhat drab office building and they rode up in a small elevator to the twelfth and highest floor.

Glass doors faced them as they emerged from the elevator, with the words *Oil Recovery Associates* emblazoned on the glass in neat gold and black letters. A receptionist, chewing gum and looking bored, sat at a semicircular desk. A half-eaten danish pastry rested at her elbow next to the telephone switchboard. Kristin stared at the pastry. Her preconceived image of secret agents and CIA buildings had no room in it for bored receptionists and half-eaten breakfasts. There was something so incongruously domestic about danish pastry.

Grey put his hand at the small of her back and ushered her forward. "Morning, Hilda. I have a nine-o'clock appointment with Mr. Smith."

"I'll confirm that, Mr. Mason." The receptionist wadded her gum into her cheek, removed a list from her desk drawer, and quickly scanned it. "Yes, your name is on the list, together with Mrs. Mason's. You can go through. Here's a badge for Mrs. Mason."

Grey took the flat plastic disk and pinned it to Kristin's jacket. They walked down a corridor that looked exactly like any other office corridor Kristin had seen. It contained several doors marked with such innocent-sounding names as *Sales Dapartment, Accounts,* and *Steno.* The room marked *Steno* had glass windows in the door, and she could see that it contained at least half a dozen women, all busy at typewriters.

"What are those women working on?" she asked.

"Probably somebody's expense account," Grey said wryly. "Or very tedious interoffice memos."

"Nobody here looks like a secret agent," she exclaimed, aware of a faint, irrational sense of disappointment. "Those women look exactly like regular typists."

Grey sounded amused. "They *are* regular typists, Kris. They work nine to five and get paid overtime if they stay late or come in over the weekend. Sometimes they get to type secret government dispatches instead of invoice sheets, but that's the only difference. In any case, I guess we work pretty hard at keeping a low profile in this division. It's only the bodyguards who go out of their way to look tough and ready for action. There seems to be some slight deterrent effect on loonies if a public figure is clearly seen to be surrounded by armed agents."

"But anybody could wander in here, Grey."

"Not quite. There are electronic sensors all along this corridor. Without the badge you're wearing, the alarm system would have been activated as soon as we passed the reception desk."

"You mean a bell would ring?"

"The alarm system in here is a little more aggressive than that," he said laconically. He pointed to the ceiling and she noticed an elaborate grid system. "Vertical steel bars would drop into position at four-foot intervals."

She glanced dubiously at the plastic disk pinned to her lapel. Even for this electronic-and-laser age, it didn't look large enough to be protecting her from such a fearful fate. She was still fingering the disk nervously when Grey halted in front of a plain wooden door. A disembodied female voice broke into the silence. "Please identify yourselves before proceeding farther."

"This is Paul Mason. My wife and I have an appointment with Mr. Smith."

"Proceed with your identification displayed in your hand, Mr. Mason."

The wooden doors slid apart to reveal a small anteroom with solid steel walls and a low steel ceiling. Kristin gulped. If the offices in the corridor had seemed disconcertingly normal, this room seemed uncomfortably like a foray into science-fiction territory.

"Who was talking?" Kristin whispered. It didn't seem appropriate to raise her voice.

"The computer. The door opens by voice and holograph scan. Unless your voiceprint is on file, the door can't be opened from this side."

Kristin gulped again as a light came on in the anteroom and the wooden doors glided to a silent close behind them. Steel doors in the wall in front of them simultaneously opened with smooth, electronic efficiency. A military policeman, machine gun in hand, stood at the entrance.

Grey's arm came out to support Kristin just in time to prevent her from stumbling over her own feet. "I'm sorry," she said faintly. "I wasn't expecting anything quite so dramatic."

The soldier examined Grey's identification carefully, then glanced at Kristin's badge. "Mr. Smith is expecting you both, sir," he said to Grey.

Yet another door confronted them. Three sets of impregnable barriers, Kristin thought wildly. She was aware that her desire to giggle was probably inspired by a mild case of hysteria. Who on earth was she going to find sitting behind all these sliding barricades? Surely it would be easier to get into the Oval Office.

Grey knocked on the remaining door, and a perfectly

normal human voice told them to come in. Kristin half expected the door to self-destruct in front of her eyes. Instead, Grey reached down and twisted a regular door-knob, standing back politely so that she could precede him into Mr. Smith's office.

A chubby man who looked like a cross between Santa Claus and one of the elves was seated behind an enormous desk. His ruddy cheeks were framed by a halo of white hair, and his eyes seemed to twinkle with welcome in the bright glow of his desk lamp. He wore a casual red sweater and a white turtleneck shirt, completing the Santa Claus image with startling exactness. Kristin began to feel that she had inadvertently wandered into a mad-house. This jolly gentleman couldn't be the dreaded Mr. Smith.

"Come in, come in. Take a seat, don't hang about at the door." His voice was rich and deep and mellow. Feeling the gentle pressure of Grey's hand at her wrist, Kristin obediently stepped forward. Grey, she noticed, didn't sit down, so she remained standing next to him.

"Good morning, sir," Grey said, his voice cool. "I'd like you to meet my wife. Kristin, this is Mr. Smith."

Mr. Smith's desk was littered with papers. With unerr-ing accuracy his fingers extracted a small sheaf of green forms from the clutter. He looked at Kristin, and there was no longer any cheerful twinkle in his eye.

"There's very little good about this morning," he said. "These are the papers you signed, Grey, authorizing the transportation of your wife from Denver to Washington. You no doubt have a good explanation for your flagrant breach of security regulations?"

"I have an excellent explanation," Grey said. "The future of my marriage was at stake. I was tired of lying to my wife, and, in any case, she no longer believed my lies."

"Then you can't have been lying very efficiently. Twelve years of government training wasted. The tax-payers will never stand for it."

"You underestimate my wife's intelligence, Smith. As Steve Callahan undoubtedly told you, she saw me at the airport last Friday. Naturally enough, none of the explanations I gave her after that seemed very satisfactory." Grey's mouth hardened into a thin, straight line. "I think you'll find I can still lie with the best of them—when my wife isn't at the receiving end of the story."

Mr. Smith grunted. He swiveled around on his chair. "You've caused a great deal of trouble, young woman."

"I'm sorry," Kristin said, although she didn't really feel particularly apologetic. She met his eyes defiantly, refusing to turn away from Mr. Smith's fierce scrutiny. "If people had told me the truth from the beginning, maybe I wouldn't have caused so many problems."

Mr. Smith grunted again, but he said nothing. Kristin found his silence as intimidating as his conversation.

"I would like permission to tell Kristin exactly what my assignment is all about," Grey said.

"Our psychological profile on her isn't favorable, you know that."

Kristin gave an involuntary jerk of protest, and Grey's fingers tightened against her waist. "I've told you repeatedly that the department is placing too much emphasis on Kristin's childhood," he said frigidly. He glanced down at her, with a hint of apology in his dark gaze. "Just because she moved around the world a lot, just because her parents left her to her own devices when she was a teenager, that doesn't mean she's likely to crack under the first hint of pressure."

"You were the one who said you had to resign from the agency when you married her."

Kristin bit back a tiny cry. Grey didn't look at her, but she saw the telltale twitch of a muscle in his jaw.

"Kristin wanted a stable, secure home life," he said. "And I guess I was ready for that, too. It was no hardship for me to leave the service. I never wanted a head-office job like Steve Callahan, and I wouldn't have come back except as a favor to the department. You wanted me on this assignment, Smith. I didn't ask for it."

Mr. Smith ignored Grey's explanation. "Her father's a Class One security risk," he said curtly.

"My father!" This time Kristin couldn't contain herself. "My father's a security risk? How can you possibly think that? It's totally ridiculous! He has no more interest in world politics than a newborn baby."

"He was born in Czechoslovakia," Mr. Smith said. "And he's returned frequently to Communist Europe to conduct symphony concerts. Last year he agreed to be a judge at the Leipzig Mozart Contest in East Germany. All the other judges were from Eastern-bloc countries."

"My father is a Mozart fanatic and is considered the world's leading expert on eighteenth-century music, which explains the Leipzig engagement. As for the rest, if you knew my father you'd realize that he'd tour at the bottom of the Atlantic Ocean if they offered him an interesting score and a well-trained orchestra to conduct. For heaven's sake, his parents left Czechoslovakia when the Nazis invaded the Sudetenland! He was six years old at the time."

"It isn't quite that simple, Kris." Grey's voice was dispassionate. "He still has relatives in Czechoslovakia. I know they're only cousins, but we have to be sure he doesn't learn anything secret, not only for his own sake, but also for the safety of people in the department. You should know how easy it is for unscrupulous governments to play upon people's family feelings. You read about incidents in the papers all the time."

"Even if what you say is true, why should telling *me* the truth about what you're doing put my father at risk?"

"I don't think it would." Grey directed a challenging look toward Mr. Smith. "My chief, however, believes you would be unable to keep the information to yourself."

Her eyes blazed with anger. "That's ridiculous!"

"Yes," said Grey. "I've said the same thing to Smith and to Callahan on numerous occasions."

Mr. Smith rested his chin on his fingers and apparently

contemplated the pile of papers in front of him. He once again looked like Santa Claus benignly reviewing a selection of Christmas toys.

"Your husband is leaving on assignment for Vienna within the next couple of days, Kristin. Your parents, I believe, are going to be there at the same time."

"You're going to Vienna?" Kristin squeaked, ignoring Smith's remark about her parents. At this precise moment, her parents' concert schedule seemed a matter of supreme indifference.

Grey nodded curtly.

"You mean you're going to the Vienna that's in Austria?" She cleared her throat, aware that her voice was still decidedly squeaky. "Wh-what are you going to do there?"

"I intend to answer my wife's questions honestly, Smith." Grey looked challengingly toward his chief, who kept his gaze fixed on the desk, shuffling his piles of papers with every appearance of consuming interest.

Grey interpreted this silence as permission to continue. He touched Kristin's arm. "Let's sit down," he said. "This may take a while."

She sank obediently into the nearest chair. In any case, her knees had begun to wobble so badly that the chair was a necessary support.

Grey loosened his tie, the only sign of tension Kristin could detect. His expression remained cool and completely composed. "The woman you saw me with at the airport on Friday is Narina Meriosova," he said. "She's a dancer. I believe she's considered to be one of the three greatest classical ballerinas performing today."

"She defected in Paris three years ago," Kristin breathed. "I saw her dance once before I met you. I thought I'd seen her somewhere before!"

"Yes, you're right. She defected when the Bolshoi Ballet was performing at the Paris Opera. It was their first stop on a world tour."

"Nureyev defected in Paris, didn't he? At the airport.

It seems to be a popular place for defections."

"Narina didn't select the place at random. Her decision to defect was carefully planned. She was—is—very happily married to a nuclear physicist working in the Soviet space program. She has a son, Grigori, who is now twelve years old. The Russians have been so embarrassed by the defection of so many of their top-flight artists and scientists that, as you probably know, all the members of a single family are rarely given permission to leave the country at the same time. In this instance, however, it seemed that an exception had been made. Her husband, Mikhail, is a very astute man. He joined the Party, made all the right friends, and the authorities had no reason to doubt his loyalty. He was given permission to attend a scientific meeting in West Germany at the same time Narina was dancing in France. Their son was given an exit visa to accompany his father. The Meriosovas realized that an opportunity like this wasn't likely to come along again in their lifetime, and the entire family planned to defect at the same time, although in different countries."

Grey fell silent.

"Something went wrong?" Kristin prompted.

"Yes. We don't know exactly what. Narina's husband is an important man. He has information and skills that would be highly valuable in our own space program, and naturally he's under more or less constant surveillance by the KGB, although he's never given them any grounds to be suspicious of his political beliefs. As I explained, he's been careful to cultivate exactly the opposite impression. Anyway, something or somebody tipped off the Soviet authorities that something was in the offing, and, with typical efficiency, the KGB canceled Grigori's exit visa and kept his father a virtual prisoner at the West German conference. Mikhail was watched twenty-four hours a day. He couldn't warn Narina about what had happened. Grigori, their son, was still in Russia, so of course Mikhail couldn't defect. Unfortunately, Narina knew nothing about any of this—how could she?—so she went ahead and defected in accordance with their original plan. She asked for political asylum, very dramatically, on stage at the Paris Opera after she'd just finished dancing *Giselle*."

"Oh, no!" Kristin's heart contracted with sympathy. "What did her husband do? He must have been frantic."

"He did the only thing he could do in the circumstances. He went back to Moscow to their nine-year-old son. They've been there together ever since. Narina hasn't seen them, spoken to them, or heard from them for three and a half years. I told you she was a very strong woman, despite her fragile appearance. I spoke the absolute truth. A weaker person couldn't have survived the mental agony she's undergone."

"You mean the Russian government won't even let her write to Grigori? To her own son? Won't they let him write to his own mother?"

"I don't know, because the Soviet authorities haven't been put to the test. I told you that Mikhail is a very smart guy. As soon as Narina defected, he made a public statement denouncing her. When he returned to Moscow, he immediately applied for a divorce, which, of course, was granted. He has voluntarily turned all her letters over to the Soviet security forces—unopened. On a couple of occasions, he's been approached by Western diplomats or reporters, and on each occasion he's launched into a long tirade about the evils of capitalism and the fact that his wife has betrayed the Revolution by choosing to live in America. The Soviet security agencies aren't easy to deceive, but Mikhail seems to have lulled their suspicions. Four months ago, he was given permission to speak at another science convention, the first time he's been allowed out of Russia since Narina defected. Three months ago, his son was granted an exit visa to go with him."

"How do you know all these details about Mikhail's plans and motives?" Kristin asked.

"When his son was granted the visa, Mikhail made contact with one of our people in Moscow. He literally took his life in his hands when he did so."

"You mean he told this person that he's planning to try to defect again? Why bother to make contact with an American agent just to say that? Why not simply go ahead and defect and avoid the risk of alerting the Soviet security forces?"

"He isn't planning to defect," Grey said quietly. "The Soviet authorities are less suspicious of him than they were, but they're not fools. The convention he's being permitted to attend isn't being held in Western Europe. It's being held in Czechoslovakia, in Prague."

"But of course he can't defect there," Kristin said. "He can't do anything in Prague! He might as well be in Russia. Czechoslovakia is just as much a Communist country as Russia is."

"I think that's debatable," Grey said. "However, it's beside the point. As I told you, Mikhail isn't planning to defect. The Czech authorities would bundle him back to Russia so fast his feet wouldn't touch the ground. He'd be in jail before nightfall, and in a mental hospital receiving 'rehabilitative treatment' before the week was out. The point is, Czechoslovakia has a border with Austria and—unlike the border between East and West Germany—this one isn't impregnable."

Kristin suddenly felt cold. Her hands were shaking, so she tucked them under her legs. "You mean Mikhail and his son are planning to make a break for it? They're going to try to escape—to cross the border into Austria?"

"Yes."

The coldness seemed to spread inward, turning her heart to ice and contracting her stomach into a freezing lump of pain.

"How are they going to do it?" Her voice cracked on the question, and she swallowed hard. "Who's going to help them?"

The silence in the office stretched out interminably.

Mr. Smith finally looked up from his papers. "Grey is going to help them, Kristin," he said. "He was deputy chief of our Prague station until he left the department. He was one of the youngest deputy chiefs of station we'd ever had. He's the only person who knows the underground route to the border."

"No!" Kristin sprang out of her chair, her hands pressed against her mouth. "No, he can't possibly go! It's too dangerous! It's insane! It's *suicide!*"

"There's no one else, Kris," Grey said quietly.

"Why not?" she demanded wildly. "What about your successor? There must be somebody else who knows this wonderful secret route of yours!"

"My successor died ten weeks ago," Grey said. "That's why I agreed to take on the assignment."

"Died? You mean, he had a heart attack or something?"

There was another lengthy silence. "No," Grey said at last. "He died while he was working on a mission. But not on this assignment. He wasn't working on this when he was killed, Kristin, I swear it."

"And that's supposed to make me feel better?" she whispered. "To know that this scheme you're talking about isn't the only crazy mission likely to kill the people working on it?"

"The mission is risky, Kristin. There's no way I can pretend otherwise." For an instant Grey's mouth softened into a smile. "You wouldn't believe me anyway. But the risks have been carefully calculated, and we believe there's a high likelihood of success."

"Terrific!" she breathed. "What does that mean? Nine chances out of ten that you make it back alive? Seven? Five?"

"The fact that your husband is conducting the mission increases the favorable odds quite significantly," Mr. Smith interjected. "That's why we asked him to come back and help us out. Two very brave people have entrusted us with their lives. We don't intend to fail them."

"Grigori is only twelve, Kris," Grey said softly. "He hasn't seen his mother for nearly four years."

"Don't! Don't do this to me!" Kristin felt sick. She sat down heavily in the chair, feeling the last remnants of color drain from her cheeks. "How are you even going to get into the country, let alone out of it? They'll arrest you at the border, Grey! You don't look a bit like a Communist worker, not even a dissident worker."

He laughed, sounding really amused. How could he laugh? she wondered. Come to that, how could he sleep, or eat, or even breathe? How had he managed to spend two months, knowing what was ahead of him, yet behaving as if nothing out of the ordinary was going on?

"I wasn't planning to saunter across the border in my jeans and running shoes," he said. "I speak Czech, Kris, you know that. You've met my family. You know that my mother's parents were born and raised in Prague. We've talked about the coincidence that we both have family from the same part of Europe."

"When we met your grandmother, you told me you spoke enough Czech to understand most of what she was saying. That's hardly the same as speaking Czech fluently enough to pass for a native."

Grey's face darkened with embarrassment. "Kris, it must be pretty obvious to you by now that I haven't been completely honest about how I've spent my time since I left school. I spent four years in Prague. I learned a lot, including how to speak fluent, colloquial Czech."

"I'm beginning to wonder if there's anything you've told me that's actually the truth."

"Most of what I've told you is true in essence, Kris. It's just the superficial details that weren't quite accurate. And you're finding out about a whole bunch of little things all at once. That's why it seems like such a lot of lies." Totally indifferent to Smith's presence, he crossed over to her side and took her in his arms. "The important truth is that I love you, Kris. I told you that the other night. Once this mission is over, I want to spend the rest

of my life being the sort of husband you want me to be.
I've never lied about wanting to make a home with you.
I've never lied about wanting to spend the rest of our
lives together. Do you believe me?"

She tipped back her head, looking directly into his
eyes. "If I asked you not to go on this mission, Grey,
what would happen?"

"Please don't ask me that, Kris." His voice was flat.

"I need to know. I think it's important for both of us
to know how you would answer me."

He turned away from her. "People's lives are at stake,"
he said. "I've been trained for this work, Kristin, just
like you've been trained to ease people's pain. I feel a—
sense of responsibility to put my special skills to work."

"I accept all that," she said. "But what if I still asked
you? What if I told you that I couldn't stand to think of
you leaving for Czechoslovakia and putting your life at
risk." Her voice sank to a whisper. "What if I told you
I didn't think I could live without you. What would you
do then, Grey?"

The room was filled with a tension that was suffo-
cating in its intensity. Grey didn't turn around, but she
could hear the sadness in his voice when he finally answered her. "If you ask me not to go to Prague, Kristin,
I won't go."

She let out her breath very slowly. His answer had
been crucial for her happiness, but she knew she should
never have thrust the question on him. In her own desperate need for reassurance, she had been cruelly unfair.
"It's all right, Grey," she said quietly. "I would never
ask you to make such an impossible choice. I do understand your obligations to the agency, you know."

He swung around, and the relief that flared in his eyes
made her hot with guilt. "Do you mean that, Kris? You
understand why I have to do this—why I haven't been
able to tell you the whole truth?"

"Yes. Now that I know what's involved, of course I
understand. I guess I've always known that things like

personal freedom and the right to free choice were important to you. It's not surprising that the agency was able to recruit you. I bet you were a very idealistic guy when you were young."

"In those long-ago days, you mean? My God, you're beginning to sound just like Steve!" Grey's laugh emerged almost as a groan. He crushed her against his body, kissing her hard. "Oh, Kris, these past couple of months have been sheer, unadulterated hell. And the last few days have been the worst of all."

Mr. Smith's dry voice intruded on their embrace with all the delicacy of an upended bucket of cold water. "Very touching. It's a scene to make an old man weep." His voice dripped irony. "I always knew that falling in love caused immediate softening of the brain, and you, Grey, seem to have a particularly acute case. Let's just hope the damage isn't irreversible. Right now you'd be about as much use on a covert operation as my pet Chihuahua."

Grey showed no particular haste to remove himself from Kristin's arms. "I didn't know you had a Chihuahua, Smith."

"I don't."

Grey smiled. "Your sarcasm isn't very subtle this morning. Once Kristin's safety has been taken care of, I guarantee there'll be no problems about my effectiveness."

"How are you expecting to take care of your wife's safety?"

Grey's gesture was dismissive. "It's easily done, Smith. You know that. Take her to a safe house. Heaven knows there are enough of them around Washington. She can stay on in the apartment I'm going to use tonight."

"Are you worried that Kristin might let something slip now that she's been informed of your mission?"

"No, of course I'm not! I'm worried about her physical safety. Didn't Steve Callahan tell you? Damon came around to the apartment while I was in Buffalo, looking for Paul Mason. There has to be a good chance he was followed, in which case far too many people know that Paul Mason and Grey Hamilton are one and the same person."

"And so?"

"Don't play silly games, Smith. I'm not in the mood. Kristin is at risk. She'd make an excellent hostage, and there's no way we can secure the Denver apartment."

Kristin interrupted the discussion, which was clearly becoming unusually heated. "You don't have to find somewhere for me to go in Washington, Mr. Smith." She spoke with a superficial calm that belied her inner turmoil. "I intend to go to Vienna with Grey."

Both men looked at her with as much astonishment as if she had just sprouted wings. "That's out of the question," Grey said flatly. "No way are you coming with me."

Mr. Smith said nothing, and, on giving him a quick second glance, Kristin realized that his eyes contained not astonishment but calculation. She began to suspect that there wasn't much she could do that would ever surprise Mr. Smith.

She drew in a deep breath, still scarcely believing what she herself had suggested. "My parents are going to be in Vienna, and I haven't seen them since the day Grey and I got married. I think it would be very natural for me to spend some time with them. In fact, I'd like to see them again."

Mr. Smith's voice was smooth. "In my opinion, Kristin, the idea has definite possibilities."

"Absolutely not," Grey said. "I refuse to allow Kristin to be involved in this operation. The subject is not open for discussion."

"I guess it's all right for you to risk your life," Kristin said softly, "but I'm not even allowed to be near you while you're doing it. Is that what you're saying, Grey?"

"You aren't accustomed to handling the sort of stress you would be subjected to in Vienna," he replied curtly.

"In the past, you haven't known what was going on, and your ignorance was the best protection you could have. That was one of the reasons I went along with Smith's insistence that you shouldn't be told anything about what I was doing. But you've forced a change in that situation by coming to Washington. You're no longer genuinely innocent, and you have no practice in feigning it. You're too honest, Kris. Your eyes are a dead giveaway. They mirror every thought you have."

"Do they? Then what am I thinking now?"

He paced impatiently across the room. "Kris, this isn't a parlor game. Take my word for it. I can't work effectively while I'm in Czechoslovakia if I have to worry the whole time that you might be blowing my cover in Vienna."

"On the other hand," Mr. Smith interjected mildly, "if Kristin manages to behave convincingly in her role as a daughter vacationing with her parents while her husband attends a science convention, your cover will be deeper and more effective."

Kristin's eyes widened. "Is that how you're getting into Czechoslovakia?" she asked. "As a delegate to the convention in Prague? You're going to cross the border openly?"

"I'm a research scientist," Grey said. "I've volunteered to read Professor Aken's latest paper to the convention. There was no difficulty in getting me a visa." He smiled, squeezing her hand very gently. "There's excellent train service between Vienna and Prague, so I decided to take advantage of it. When I hit my twenty-ninth birthday, I kind of gave up on crawling under barbed-wire fences. At least if there were any more comfortable alternatives."

She closed her eyes in involuntary rejection of the images his words conjured up. His tone was teasing, but she wasn't deceived as to the dangers involved. "But once you get into Prague, how in the world are you going to get out? When the authorities realize Mikhail and

Grigori are missing, every security officer in the country is going to be looking for them. And for you, if you're missing at the same time."

"Kris, don't worry about things," Grey said softly. "Bureaucracies aren't all that efficient, not even in Communist countries. In fact, especially not in Communist countries. You simply have to understand their systems and work around them. There are fifteen million people in Czechoslovakia. That's a pretty big haystack for three people to lose themselves in. Don't worry, I have a perfectly adequate escape plan worked out."

"What? Tell me what you'll do!"

"You know I can't do that, Kris." He grinned. "But no crawling under barbed wire, I promise. I'll come back without a scratch on my elegant surface."

She got to her feet, feeling a little surprised by her own determination to go to Vienna. For once Grey wasn't going to turn her aside with laughter and teasing and persuasion. Knowing that he was in danger was going to be hard enough. Biting her nails in some government apartment in Washington would make the wait intolerable. She wondered briefly what had happened to the old Kristin, the woman who craved security and stability and a quiet home life. She appeared to have vanished.

"I'm coming with you, Grey," she said. "I'm your wife and I want to share as much of this with you as I can."

"Please understand, Kris, that I want your company, but I can't risk taking you. I can't go off on this mission leaving a frantic wife behind in Vienna."

"I thought you were the man who told Smith and Callahan that I wouldn't crack under pressure," Kristin said. "Why do you assume I would be frantic? It's not very flattering of you."

He ran his hand distractedly through his thick hair. "Don't push, Kris."

Mr. Smith stood up. He was tall, Kristin realized, and, despite his chubby cheeks, his body was trim and in first-rate condition. The impression of jolly old Santa Claus wavered, then vanished completely when he spoke. This was a man well accustomed to command, she realized, and ruthless in achieving his objectives. His role in the interview had been low-key so far simply because he hadn't made up his mind.

He walked around his desk, perching on the corner with a casualness that was only skin-deep. "I believe Kristin should go to Austria," he said. "Your powers of concentration will be no better, Grey, whether you've left your wife behind in Washington or Vienna."

"Is that a direct order, Smith?"

"Something like that."

"I would like to know why you consider Kristin's presence in Vienna desirable." There was a distinct pause. "Sir."

"As you know perfectly well, Grey, Narina Meriosova flew from Washington to London last Saturday. She's dancing there with the Royal Ballet. She leaves for Vienna in two days' time to make a guest appearance at the Vienna Opera House. Those engagements were set up six months ago, long before any of us knew about her husband's plans for escape. After considerable debate—in which, you may remember, you took an active part—we decided it's less suspicious for Meriosova to keep those engagements than it is for her to cancel them. It's a great misfortune that she'll be in Vienna. Her story has attracted an enormous amount of publicity in Europe, more than it has here, for some reason, and some smart-ass reporter is absolutely certain to come up with the fact that her former husband is a major speaker at the convention in Prague. Once that fact becomes public knowledge, it's going to be only a matter of time before the press descends on her in its usual vulturelike fashion, asking what it feels like to know that her twelve-year-old son is only a hundred and fifty miles away."

"I'm well aware of the difficulties of Narina's position, Smith. What does this have to do with Kristin?"

"She's the daughter of two world-famous musicians and an extremely logical companion for Narina Meriosova. Not a single eyebrow would be raised anywhere if they spent a great deal of their free time together. Kristin also happens to be one of the very few people who know what's actually going on. Hell, she's dealt with journalists and press interviews since she was a small child. She can help shield Narina from the worst of the newshounds. More important, when Narina needs a shoulder to cry on, Kristin will be there, already knowing the truth. Having Kristin around means that there will be one person in Vienna that Narina doesn't have to pretend with. I think that's going to be a big help. In my professional judgment, the advantages outweigh the risks, which are slight."

"I gather you've revised your previous opinion of Kristin's psychological strength." Again the slight pause. "Sir."

Mr. Smith looked long and hard at Grey. "Yes, I have. It was you yourself who misled me, you know. You were so protective that naturally I assumed there was some fundamental weakness in her that needed protection."

For the first time that morning a hint of a genuine smile tugged at Smith's mouth. "I suspect the only failing I have as a judge of character is my tendency to forget the devastating effect of being in love on the human powers of reason."

"Your modesty is overwhelming, Smith."

"Modesty isn't a very useful characteristic in my job. Confidence in my own judgment is." Mr. Smith levered himself away from his perch on the desk and pressed a button on his telephone console, before speaking into it. "Grey Hamilton is booked on a Lufthansa flight to Vienna tomorrow night, via Frankfurt. Get me another seat on the same plane, will you? For Mrs. Grey Hamilton."

He waited for an acknowledgment of his instructions, then nodded briskly toward Kristin. "Do you have your passport with you?"

"Oh, no! I don't even have a passport in my married name."

"No problem. Ask Hilda, the receptionist, to take a couple of pictures before you leave. Grey will bring the passport home with him this evening."

Grey put his arm around her and drew her into a corner of the room. With surprising tact, Mr. Smith turned away from them and busied himself with a prolonged search through one of his filing cabinets.

"Kristin, are you sure about this?" Grey asked. "You don't have to do anything you don't want to do, you know. I have enough authority simply to refuse to take you."

"I *want* to come with you to Vienna," she said. She reached out to caress the rigid line of his jaw, aching to soothe away the tension she sensed in him but not sure how. "While Mr. Smith was talking, I realized something important about our relationship, Grey: You've been too kind to me. You've humored me and teased me gently whenever we've hit any sort of rough spot. Do you remember what you said after the Akens came to dinner last week?"

He nuzzled her nose. "Obviously something very profound. What was it?"

"You told me that I tend to take people too much at surface value, and you were right. Living with my parents, I met literally hundreds of different people, and I learned it was easier to cope with them if I didn't try to get to know them as individuals. If they were pleasant to me, I was pleasant back. If they were difficult or hard to get along with, I avoided them. I fell in love with you, Grey, almost the first time we met, but even so I've never allowed myself to look too hard or too closely at our relationship. You made it easy—too easy—for me to be selfish. Ever since we met, you've consistently put my needs above your own. I realize now what you've been doing: You've tried to make up for every time my parents ever uprooted me or ignored me or put my wishes in second place to theirs. Well, it's not necessary to spoil me anymore. I want a husband, not a substitute father-figure. And that means I want to share your problems as well as your good times. I want a lover and a friend, not just a protector."

Grey buried his face in her hair and tightened his arms around her, enclosing her in his strength even as he revealed his own vulnerability. "I think we're doing pretty well in the lover department," he said softly. "But I guess maybe we could work a little harder on becoming friends."

Before she could reply, Kristin felt a firm tap on her shoulder. "These touching scenes are getting to me," Mr. Smith said. "I've never seen so much passion in this office before. However, I think it's time we all floated down from our romantic clouds and got back to work."

He tightened his grip on her shoulder, propelling her toward the door with brisk authority. "Grey has a heavy schedule this afternoon," he said, "but I'll try to see that he gets home at a reasonable hour. And then please take him to bed and make love to him for the rest of the night. For God's sake, let's do something to get his hormones back in balance before he goes to Prague."

Kristin smiled. "Is that an order, Mr. Smith?"

"Definitely. Give him a workover and clear his sinuses, or his glands, or whatever it is that's softening his brain." Without any pause to indicate his change of subject, Smith continued. "Hilda will arrange for a car and driver to take you back to where you're staying tonight. If you have any shopping you need to do before you leave for Vienna, please tell the driver. He'll stop en route for you. Once you're in the apartment, you won't be able to leave."

She didn't bother to inquire precisely what electronic locking system would keep her housebound. After the revelations of the past couple of days, it seemed almost too trivial a detail to pursue.

Grey opened the door of Mr. Smith's office and said good-bye to her as she entered the steel-lined anteroom with its military guard. On second acquaintance she decided that the soldier looked almost friendly, as long as she remembered not to look down the barrel of his machine gun.

She hurried back to the reception desk, smiling a touch nervously as she greeted Hilda. The receptionist returned her smile, and Kristin felt a surge of excitement as she explained about her need for passport photos. Tomorrow night she was going to fly to Austria! She was going to spend twenty-four hours with Grey in one of the most beautiful cities in Europe. Provided she didn't think about what would happen after he left her, it promised to be a magical twenty-four hours.

With a somewhat wry smile, she followed the young man who had arrived to take her photograph. Her stay in Vienna wasn't going to be all moonlight and roses, but, whatever way she looked at it, it sure beat the heck out of a weekend in Buffalo.

Chapter Ten

KRISTIN HAD NO opportunity to fulfill Mr. Smith's instructions regarding Grey's hormone balance. Far from arriving at the apartment at a reasonable hour, it was almost two in the morning when he finally came in. Kristin was already in bed, although not asleep.

"Is everything all right?" she asked anxiously as he slipped into bed beside her.

"A couple of last-minute problems. Just something minor. Everything's straightened out now." He reached for her while he was speaking, folding her into the curves of his body and stroking her hair with a soft sigh of pleasure. Within thirty seconds he was asleep.

Their flight didn't take off from Washington until the late afternoon, but Grey didn't sleep in. His alarm went off at six, and he dressed quickly, not bothering to eat breakfast before he left. He kissed Kristin good-bye, his expression apologetic as he left the apartment.

"I still have a few loose ends to tie up," he said. "Don't worry. I'll be back in plenty of time to make the plane. Do you have something to do while I'm gone? A book to read or something?"

With a phenomenal exercise of willpower, she replied that she had two books to read and a program on wildlife that she wanted to watch on the public television channel. She resisted the impulse to demand that he tell her what "minor" problems were causing so much last-minute activity. She watched him leave, feeling her heart pound heavily with anxiety. She then spent the morning pacing the apartment, wondering how on earth she was going to get through twenty-four hours alone with him in Austria without breaking down and begging him hysterically not to leave for Prague.

It was cool and misty when they landed in Vienna after fifteen hours of travel. They had spent only nine hours in the air; the rest of their time had dragged by slowly as they waited out delays in the departure lounges of Washington and Frankfurt airports. Kristin was exhausted. It was amazing, she reflected as she and Grey displayed their passports to a friendly Austrian immigration officer, that departure lounges the world over could manage to look so similar and so discouragingly impersonal. It was as if some giant international company with an overstock of orange carpeting had been asked to decorate all the world's airports. She found the effect of so much vibrant color on her jet-lagged system less than soothing, but she managed to smile as the immigration official returned her passport and politely welcomed her to Austria. Her smile turned into a smothered yawn.

"Tired?" Grey asked.

"Mmm. I'm not good at crossing time zones. My body is telling me in no uncertain terms that it's still night in Denver, and I'm supposed to be tucked into bed."

"Me, too. I keep fantasizing about swirling bubble

baths and soft beds with down comforters. Not to mention big, fat, feather pillows."

She smiled. "Sounds wonderfully erotic."

"Honey, unless you find deep sleep erotic, I'm afraid not. I think it's touch and go whether I'll make it out of the bathroom and into the bed before I fall asleep."

They took a cab to the Bristol, the luxurious hotel opposite the Opera House where Kristin's parents always stayed when they were in Vienna. They checked in quickly, entering their room on the seventh floor with joint sighs of relief. Neither of them attempted to unpack. Kristin stripped off her clothes, and Grey ran water for a bath. He hadn't been exaggerating his tiredness, Kristin realized a few minutes later when she went into the bathroom. He was fast asleep in a cocoon of scented aquamarine foam. She shook him awake, and he stayed conscious just long enough to wrap himself in a towel, walk into the bedroom, and collapse on the bed. He immediately fell back to sleep.

Kristin took a brief shower, and two minutes later was curled up next to him on the giant bed. She was conscious of nothing more until she woke to a darkened room and the sounds of a Viennese waltz playing quietly over the radio.

She opened one eye and saw Grey sitting on the edge of the bed. "Hi," he said, rumpling her hair. "I thought we'd better get up. It's dinnertime."

The soft feather bed was the most comfortable thing Kristin had ever felt in her life. She burrowed deeper into the linen-covered down comforter and closed her eye.

"No dinner," she mumbled. "Not hungry. I want to sleep."

He tickled her cheek, preventing her from drifting back into the blissful mists of slumber. "You'll wake up at two in the morning with raging insomnia and an even more raging appetite. And at that hour, there'll be nowhere to eat. Come on, Kris. I've booked a table in the hotel dining room. I read my guidebook, and it says this hotel has one of Europe's most glittering and sophisti-cated restaurants. Outstanding Viennese cuisine. There are four little stars right next to the name of the chef."

Kristin opened both eyes this time so that she could glare at him more effectively. "Did I ever tell you that I hate people who are as cheerful as you are when they wake up?"

He patted her affectionately on the bottom. "I think you may have mentioned it once or twice. Probably not more than a hundred times since we got married."

She groaned, then sat up with decided reluctance. "Grey, right now I don't feel in the least bit glittering and sophisticated. Couldn't we order something from room service if you're really hungry?"

"On our first night in Vienna? How can you be so pedestrian? Besides, I've already called down to the res-taurant and booked a table for eight o'clock. Once we're actually ordering dinner, you'll be glad I persuaded you to get up. You'll see. Just think of all those fabulous cakes and pastries that they serve for dessert here. They're enough to entice anybody out of bed."

She groaned again. "Aha! The truth at last. Now I understand why I'm being dragged downstairs. *You* want to eat chocolate and whipped cream, so *I'm* being forced to get up!"

"Not at all," he said, feigning offended dignity. "I'm simply giving you a unique opportunity to indulge your-self. Surely even you will admit to being tempted by the idea of puff pastry covered with chocolate fudge, layered with walnuts and fresh whipped cream, topped by can-died black cherries and curls of chocolate. I understand that's the specialty of the hotel restaurant."

"I suppose your guidebook told you all that, too?"

He nodded, his smile teasing.

"All right, you win, Grey! Only a full-fledged mas-ochist could resist a dessert like that." Laughing, she turned back the comforter and pulled herself off the bed.

She went into the bathroom and took another swift shower, letting the water run almost cold. She needed something radical to jerk her protesting body into alertness.

She knew European restaurants were usually more formal than their American counterparts, which made choosing an outfit relatively easy. She had packed only one dinner dress, a silk and wool fabric in dusty pink, and she slipped it on quickly, coiling her blond hair loosely on top of her head. She softened the severity of the style by leaving a few wisps to curl against her cheeks, and by wearing a pair of drop pearl earrings. She brushed tinted gloss across her mouth and darkened her long lashes with mascara, then put on high-heeled gray sandals and picked up a slim gray leather purse. She examined the finished product in the floor-length mirror by the door. Her reflection looked strangely unfamiliar, she decided, more delicate and yet somehow more vibrant, more vividly alive, than she remembered herself being.

She turned away from the mirror, uncomfortably aware of a sense of disorientation. Events had moved so rapidly that it was as if part of her had been left behind in their Denver apartment, still waiting to catch up with the other part of her that had already flown several thousand miles across the Atlantic to Austria.

Grey came out of the bathroom at that moment, and she turned toward him somewhat hesitantly. "You look more than glittering and sophisticated," he said huskily. "You look ravishing, Kris. Literally."

She gazed at him mischievously. "More enticing than chocolate cake with nuts and cherries?"

He grinned. "Very nearly, although after deep consideration I guess the chocolate cake wins out. But only by a narrow margin, Kris, I promise."

She smiled wryly. "What in the world do you do with all those calories you consume, Grey?"

"Burn them up in nervous tension, I think." His reply was utterly casual and perhaps not even intended seriously, but Kristin felt an uncomfortable chill ripple down her spine. She tugged self-consciously at the neckline of her dress, suddenly not at all sure what to say next.

She knew Grey picked up on her change of mood. "Let's go downstairs," he said softly. "I want to show you off and make all the other men in the restaurant jealous."

The baroque elegance of the dining room took Kristin's breath away. She had stayed at the Bristol with her parents when she was a little girl, but she had no memory of eating with them in such elegant surroundings. She and Grey spent some time examining the lengthy menu. When they had finally ordered thin pancakes stuffed with veal and mushrooms, and a bottle of dry white wine that came from the Wachau area along the Danube, Grey leaned back in his chair. He looked at her searchingly.

"Do you want to leave a message for your parents, Kris, to let them know you've arrived in Vienna?"

She was looking forward to seeing her parents again, but she had no doubt about her answer. "No," she said. "Thanks for asking, Grey, but I want us to have this time alone together. I'll get in touch with my parents as soon as you've—when you've left for the convention."

She was much more sensitive to his moods now than she had been in the past, and she sensed the relaxation within him of some indefinable tension.

"That's good news," he said simply. "I'm looking forward to touring the city with you tomorrow. What do you think we should see first?"

They discussed their schedule for the following day over a superb meal. By unspoken consent, they made no reference to their real reason for being in Vienna and no reference to the fact that, by this time the next day, Grey would be preparing to leave for Czechoslovakia. They both ate their entire portion of the unbelievably rich dessert, accompanied by strong, fragrant cups of black coffee. Kristin left the restaurant feeling deliciously overfed, and with the rueful suspicion that this might become her permanent condition for as long as she stayed in Vienna.

"Let's take a walk around," Grey suggested. "It's too early to go back to the room."

She was happy to agree. The earlier clouds had entirely disappeared, and the night air was clean and crisp. Their hotel was close to Vienna's most fashionable shopping district and the lighted window displays glowed enticingly in the darkness. They walked without any particular destination in mind, stopping every now and then to admire an elegant display of woolen goods or embroidered linens.

It was late when they finally returned to their room. Kristin kicked off her sandals and tossed her purse on the dressing table, sighing with pleasure as Grey pulled her down onto the bed.

"Have you ever noticed what a wonderful place bed is?" she asked, wriggling with enjoyment on the puffy comforter.

Grey tickled her gently across the ribs, then lifted her up so that he could reach the zipper of her dress. He pushed it slowly downward. The night air felt cool, almost caressing against her skin.

"Honeybun," he murmured, "I hope that isn't a tactful way of saying you're feeling sleepy. Those refreshing breezes from the Danube seem to have done something extraordinary to my libido."

He leaned possessively over her, and she glanced up at him, her eyes brimming with laughter. "It seems to have done something pretty extraordinary to other parts of your anatomy as well."

"That isn't the Danube," he said, rubbing his body erotically against her thighs. "That's you. It's always you, Kristin." His mouth moved to cover hers, sealing it with a teasing kiss. They were both startled when the kiss exploded into a blaze of hot, searching passion, all the more intense because it contained somewhere within it the bittersweet awareness that soon they would be parted.

With a low moan of need Kristin pulled him closer,

weaving her fingers through his hair and moving her lips urgently beneath his. She clung to him in surrender, wanting to tell him how much she loved him, how desperately she needed him to come back safely from his mission. But his impassioned kisses and skilled hands turned her mind into a fathomless pool of darkness and her body into a helpless, flooding river of desire. She couldn't even form coherent sentences, let alone speak them out loud.

She had no memory of removing her clothes. One minute she and Grey were both dressed; the next minute they were lying naked together, cushioned in the billowing folds of the comforter. Grey's lovemaking quickly brought her to the shimmering brink of ecstasy. She hovered there for one soaring, shining moment before they collapsed together into the sharp, sweet union of a shared climax.

They remained curled in each other's arms for a long time, their bodies momentarily replete, their heartbeats gradually slowing. Finally, after a long while, he leaned over and kissed her eyelids, tucking the tangled strands of her hair behind her ears.

"We'll have to search the bed for hairpins," he said, his voice tinged with laughter. "Otherwise we might discover them the hard way!"

She touched her earlobes. "I lost my earrings, too. We mustn't forget to look for them. They belonged to my grandmother."

She turned toward him, nestling more comfortably into the hollow of his shoulder. She ran her hand across his chest, following the dark line of his hair down the length of his body.

"Grey," she said, "tell me how you first got started with the agency."

"There's not much to tell..."

She reached out and stroked his jaw, holding her fingers against his mouth to stop his denials. "Please, Grey. I want to know."

He moved a little away from her, propping himself up against the headboard as he started to speak. "It's not that interesting a story, but if you really want to know..."

She nodded. "I really want to know."

"Well, I guess I was as uninterested in politics as any other teenager, until I was about sixteen. That's when my father went to work for the Commerce Department. After a few months in Washington, he was assigned to the embassy in Bonn, where he had responsibility for encouraging U.S. exports to West Germany. He helped American businessmen to understand the European markets and pointed out special opportunities for export. You know the sort of thing."

"Mmm. But I didn't know you'd lived in Germany when you were a child."

"I never did live there. My dad went to Bonn by himself. It was only a two-year assignment, and my mother stayed in the States with me and my sister. We were both in high school, and she was very much opposed to the idea of disrupting our education. In any case, I don't think she and my father ever had a very close relationship. He's been running his own leather goods factory for years, but they still don't seem to do much together if they can avoid it. Anyway, my sister and I stayed in Colorado during the school year with my mom, but she decided to send us to Europe during the summer vacation. She said it would be educational."

When Grey fell silent, Kristin prompted, "And was it?"

He grimaced with wry humor. "In more ways than one. I had a great time in Bonn. I fell in love with a cute German girl who was determined to do her best for transatlantic relations by personally undertaking my sexual education. I'd spent a lot of time playing football and not much time dating girls, so Klara had a great deal to teach me."

Kristin's voice was very dry. "Somehow I suspect you made a brilliant pupil for dear little Klara."

There was a touch of embarrassment in his smile. "I think Klara was probably a first-rate tease. I seem to remember a lot of hot hands and heavy breathing in the back of her parents' Volkswagen, but not much else. Anyway, as you can imagine, I decided Bonn was a fabulous place to spend a vacation, and I was mad as fire when my dad announced that we were all taking a trip to Berlin. He had business there, and he thought my sister and I could learn something from the experience."

"And something happened there? Something important?"

"I was pretty bored by Berlin," Grey said slowly. "There was no Klara. No heavy breathing in the Volkswagen. We'd been there three days, and it had rained the whole time. I didn't want to go shopping and was fed up with traipsing around museums. I told my dad I was too old to be taken to the zoo, and he said I was too young to go to any of the nightclubs. All in all, the whole place seemed drab and colorless and cold, and it depressed the heck out of me. I wasn't interested in memorials to soldiers killed during World War II, and, as far as I could see, the whole place was virtually one giant war memorial. The Vietnam issue was just heating up in the States around that time, and I, like the rest of the kids in my high school class, basically thought that war was a rotten idea and always unjustified. The only political belief I had was that Americans ought not to be getting killed in some lousy jungle in Southeast Asia. As far as I was concerned, all government systems seemed more or less the same. One government was as corrupt as another, and the ordinary citizen got screwed whether he lived in a democracy or a dictatorship." He smiled faintly. "If you remember, the late sixties were a pretty radical time for young Americans."

"I was in grade school. I don't really remember much of it all. My impressions mostly come from documentaries on television."

"In retrospect, I can see that it was a tough period to

be a parent. If you sent your son to college, the chances were good he'd end up spending his time inciting riots. If you didn't send him to college, he got drafted and shipped off to Asia. It wasn't only my dad who was struggling to make sense of it all. I think in some way he was hoping that, seeing Berlin, we might understand what the division in the world was all about. Of course, we didn't. Anyway, the last day we were in Berlin, it finally stopped raining, and my dad took us for a walk along the Wall. There are twenty-eight miles of it, and for a while I was afraid he was going to make us go the entire distance. He was lecturing us the whole time. I agreed with him that it was terrible a city should be divided, but I couldn't understand why he was so worked up about the whole thing."

Grey put his hands behind his head and stared reflectively at the old-fashioned plaster ceiling, his eyes shadowed with uncomfortable memories.

"I guess teenagers have a natural tendency to be selfish or foolish or both. I was probably no worse than most other seventeen-year-olds. I like to think that, anyway."

Kristin stroked a series of reassuring circles on his stomach. "I expect most seventeen-year-old boys are like most seventeen-year-old girls. Ninety percent of their energy is devoted to thinking about sex. The remaining ten percent of their attention has to cover a whole lot of topics, so sometimes their attention gets stretched a bit thin."

Grey's smile remained shadowed. "All the time we were walking along, I kept hoping my dad would quit with the lecture and decide we'd had enough education for the day. Suddenly a group of people in front of us started shouting. I looked up and saw a man screaming something and pointing to the Wall. I don't know how all the locals knew something was going to happen. Maybe they heard noises from the other side; maybe they could recognize when the border guards got ready for action. Maybe the whole thing was prearranged, I don't know.

My dad started to run, and we ran after him, toward the crowd of people. Then, all at once, the border guards began shooting—great wild bursts of machine-gun fire—and at the same time we saw a woman's head peer over the top of the Wall. Her hands were clawing at the edges, pulling desperately although there's broken glass stuck all the way along the top. She was shrieking something, but of course I couldn't understand what because I didn't speak German. She finally managed to heave herself up, and I saw that she had a bundle hanging around her neck. She tore at it frantically, then tossed it straight into the hands of somebody waiting in the crowd on our side of the Wall. I think she must already have been wounded, because she never made it any farther. She just fell back down and disappeared on her side of the Wall. You could tell where she'd tried to make it over, though, because the bricks were soaked with blood. My dad and my sister and I finally reached the point where she'd tried to escape, and we saw what she'd thrown over."

He was silent for so long that Kristin finally had to ask him, "What was it?"

"It was a baby," he said. "A toddler, actually. I found out later that it was a little girl. I suppose the mother had been screaming for somebody to catch her baby; that's why all the people had gone running. You know, when I looked at those great streaks of blood and heard that little girl yelling her lungs out while all the West Berliners tried to comfort her, it finally occurred to me that there must be differences between government systems if people were prepared to risk their lives to get from one side of the Wall to the other. For the first time I thought about what it must be like to live under a government that needs to build a twenty-eight-mile-long wall to keep its citizens within its boundaries."

"Was the baby hurt?"

"No. By some miracle she'd escaped all the machine-gun fire, the glass shards, everything. They found a note pinned to her undershirt, giving her name and explaining that her father had been jailed for printing an illegal newspaper. He was doing twenty years of hard labor somewhere in the mountains."

"What was the baby's name?"

"Klara." Grey's laugh was hard. "Do you know, that unimportant coincidence bothered me more than anything else. I couldn't put it out of my mind—the contrast between Klara, giggling while we made out in the back of the Volkswagen, and the baby Klara, crying her heart out while her mother threw her over a wall."

Kristin shuddered, instinctively moving closer to him. "Heavens, Grey, that was a traumatic experience for a teenager."

"Yes. My sister went away to college as soon as we got back to the States, and we never really talked about the incident until years later. Then she finally admitted to me that she'd had nightmares about it the whole time she was in college. I didn't have nightmares, but I sometimes felt like I was the only student on campus who wasn't out in the streets protesting against U.S. involvement in Vietnam. I wasn't sure that I was in favor of having troops there, you know, but I just couldn't bring myself to protest either. That's probably why Steve Callahan first decided to recruit me."

"Steve Callahan recruited you?"

"Yes. We told you the truth the other night. We were at Georgetown University together, but the graduate courses we took were a cover for our real training with the agency, which was going on concurrently. Eventually we were both sent overseas. I remained on overseas station until eighteen months ago, just before I met you."

"Why do some people know you as Paul Mason?"

"A couple years ago I needed to spend a few months in Washington while things cooled off in Europe. I had a cover job at the Commerce Department, supposedly evaluating export licenses for energy systems. Paul Mason was my alias at the agency, and I used it for the Commerce Department job. We were very careful to keep

Paul Mason's life entirely separate from Grey Hamilton's, but unfortunately a few people recently have begun to connect the two people. It doesn't really matter. Once this assignment is over, Paul Mason can be buried for good."

"But what about your family, Grey? Did they know about all this? Didn't they wonder where you were and what you were doing over in Europe?"

"No, there was no reason for them to wonder. I told them I was working overseas for the Commerce Department. Dad had done that for a short while, so it seemed very believable. In fact, they boasted to all their friends about the marvelous job I'd landed right out of college. I visited them whenever I came back to the States, and the agency forwarded their letters to me."

His expression became dark and somewhat brooding. "I've learned that it's frighteningly easy to deceive people who trust you. When you love somebody, you want to believe that they're telling the truth, and I was trained to take advantage of that trust. I did it with you, Kristin, as well as with my parents and sister."

"I'll make sure you remember your guilt feelings," she said. "While you're gone, I'll spend time dreaming up suitable ways to punish you for deceiving me. How about a month's confinement to a narrow bed in a locked room?"

"Sounds fantastic," he said. "As long as you go with the bed."

"It's a deal." She yawned, stirring against him in drowsy content. "Grey, you remember when you came to consult me at the hospital, the first time we met?"

"Yes."

"Those bruises—had you really fallen downstairs?"

She saw the sudden gleam of his smile in the darkness. "No, I was on a parachute jump, and the chute didn't open properly. I landed in a tree."

"Oh, my God! Were you on a mission? Were you in terrible danger?"

"Only of ruptured eardrums. It was a training session, and the sergeant who was conducting the exercise didn't believe my story of a faulty operating mechanism on the chute. He climbed up the tree where I'd landed just so he could be right on hand to tell me what he thought of my rotten jump. His vocabulary was colorful in the extreme. I learned several valuable new words and phrases."

She laughed. "Couldn't you pretend you were unconscious or something and arouse his sympathy?"

"I tried that. But when he started throwing me over his shoulder to carry me down to the ground, I decided it was time to wake up. Insults were a better choice than being banged down twenty feet of tree trunk. And, believe me, the sergeant wasn't in the mood to treat me gently."

She nuzzled her lips against the roughness of his cheek. His beard was already starting to grow again. "I always knew you weren't clumsy enough to fall downstairs," she said. "That was a stupid story."

"I have a better one to tell you," he murmured, a husky edge to his voice. "Have you heard the one about the secret agent who thought he might vanish into the Austrian sunset if his wife didn't make love to him?"

Her laughter faded, changing swiftly to passion as he drew her body tenderly against his. She began to respond eagerly to his lovemaking, then abruptly she pushed herself a little way out of his arms.

"Grey, tonight please let's not take any birth-control precautions," she said. "I want to have your baby so much. Let me try to get pregnant tonight."

He was silent for a long time, then he drew her back into his embrace, ignoring her wriggles of protest. "Kris, please don't tempt me," he said. "When Smith asked me to help out with this mission, one of my first reactions was relief because you weren't pregnant. I very much want you to have my child, and I've spent a lot of time daydreaming about watching our baby grow inside you. But daydreams are one thing, and reality is another.

When I force myself to think about our situation logically, I know it's not sensible for you to get pregnant right now."

"I'm not sure people should depend entirely on logic when they think about having children," she said. She spoke softly, deliberately attempting to lighten the mood. "Anybody who's spent much time around teenagers knows that—logically speaking—it's insane to become a parent. Who in their right mind would voluntarily choose to share their home with a typical teenager? Yet people do it all the time. Heck, some people even volunteer to be foster parents."

"You know that isn't what I mean, Kris."

"I know. But whatever happens to you during the next few days, I could never regret having your child. If something . . . if anything happens to you, your baby wouldn't suddenly become an unwanted burden. It would be even more important to me because it would be part of you."

His hands tightened against her, and he reached up and brushed his thumb lovingly across her lips. "It isn't only our own feelings we have to consider," he said. "If I make you pregnant, that means there's automatically a third person involved in all our decisions. If you get pregnant, it means we're creating another human being who has wants and needs of his own, but no power to express them. I've always thought a baby is entitled to two parents if he can possibly get them. I know sometimes things don't work out that way, but I don't feel I have the right to have a child when I may not be around to care for him. You'd be a terrific mother, Kris, but a mother is only half of the equation. Kids need fathers, too."

"Everything you're saying sounds terrific and thoughtful and wonderfully responsible, but it doesn't take account of *our* needs . . . of the way I feel." She swallowed hard over the sudden lump of tears in her throat. "I want your baby, Grey, and I have a terrible feeling you're trying to protect me when I don't need protection. Surely, even if they haven't done anything else, these last few days have proven to you that I don't need to have everything in my life made smooth and easy. I'm strong enough to cope with being a one-parent family."

"I realize that." Grey's body was very still, and he turned his head away from her so she couldn't see his face. "Don't you see, Kris? It's not you I'm trying to protect, it's myself."

"I don't understand..."

"When I go into Czechoslovakia, I'll need a hundred percent of my concentration if I'm going to help Mikhail and Grigori to safety. I've agreed to take on the job, so now it's my responsibility to see that the job gets done. For however long it takes to bring this mission off, I have to put you out of my mind completely. That's already an almost impossible task, and if I left here knowing that you might be pregnant with my child, it would become totally impossible."

His voice faded to a husky whisper. "I need your help, Kris. I only have so much willpower. If you ask me again to make you pregnant, I won't be able to say no. So please, Kris, don't ask me."

He had always seemed so strong, so emotionally invulnerable, that she was startled by his admission. Realizing just how much his confession must have cost him, she felt her heart contract with a surge of love. She still regretted his decision and didn't entirely agree with the reasoning behind it, but she knew it would be wrong to push the issue any further. Sometimes in a marriage you had to lose the battle in order to win the war.

She knelt at his side, brushing a soft kiss at the corner of his mouth. "I love you," she said. "Just make sure you come back from Czechoslovakia with everything in perfect working condition. That's an order."

He laughed, then turned quickly, pulling her body beneath his and capturing her lips in a long, hard kiss.

"You'll have my baby soon, Kris, I promise you."

His mouth moved over her skin, leaving a trail of fire wherever it passed. "When I come back from Prague, we'll lock ourselves in that bedroom you mentioned and refuse to come out until you're pregnant. How does that sound?"

"Exhausting. I'd better start getting in training."

He tickled her stomach gently. "If you'd only stop eating all that health food, you'd have more stamina. When we get back to the States, I'm going to start a campaign to get carrot juice declared illegal. No man should have to watch his wife drinking carrot juice across the breakfast table."

She was smiling when his mouth descended to take hers, stifling the laughter at the same time that it stifled the little lingering ache of regret. His body moved against hers in an intoxicating rhythm, and she felt herself melt into an inevitable surrender.

Tomorrow night he won't be here.

She pushed the black thought out of her mind. At least for tonight she had his arms around her and his body joined tightly to hers. For tonight, perhaps that was all she needed.

Chapter Eleven

THE FIRST THING she saw when she woke up late the next morning was the note propped against the dressing-table mirror. She unfolded it carefully, smoothing out its folds as if she were afraid it might crumble beneath the touch of her fingers. Grey's message was short.

In the end, it seemed more convenient to travel to the convention by bus, so I had to leave Vienna earlier than we'd originally planned. Sorry I couldn't tell you in person.

The conference lasts four days, did I already mention that? Take care of yourself, and remember that chocolate is good for the soul if not for the digestion. Carrot juice is bad for everything except night vision, and who needs to see in the dark? I love you. Grey.

She read the note three times, but its message re-

mained the same. Grey had gone—and he had deliberately avoided saying good-bye.

She put the note into her purse, then showered and
dressed and went down to breakfast, carefully closing
her mind to any worries about where Grey might be at
this precise moment and what he might be doing. She
didn't even know when he had left, she thought as she
waited for the waiter to bring her breakfast. Ten minutes
after they had made love? An hour before she woke up
this morning? She pushed the useless speculation aside
and ate her meal, then went straight to the reception desk.
She had made a great many promises about helping Grey
if she was allowed to accompany him to Vienna. She
owed it to herself to live up to those promises.

"I would like to visit with Frederick and Anne Marie
Nordwald," she said to the dark-suited male receptionist.
"Could you please tell me their suite number?"

"I will be happy to telephone their room, Fräulein,
and tell them you wish to see them. Your name, please?"

"Kristin Hamilton. I'm their daughter. I sent them a
cable from the States, so they should be expecting me."

The receptionist retreated to a telephone at some distance from the counter to place his call. He returned a
few minutes later, smiling politely as he directed her to
the top floor of the hotel. "Your parents are looking
forward to seeing you, Fräulein."

She was a bit surprised to find that her mouth was
dry and her stomach churning when she knocked on the
cream-painted door of her parents' suite. The door was
immediately flung open, and her mother greeted her with
a lilting cry, her arms stretched wide and high in a dramatic gesture of welcome.

Kristin recognized the gesture of old. She had seen it
on the stage many times. Princess Aïda, she thought with
a touch of unusual cynicism, welcoming home the Captain of the Imperial Egyptian Army.

Despite the theatricality of the pose, her mother's
smile seemed genuinely radiant, and her voice, when she

finally spoke, was as sweet and beautiful as ever. "Darling, Kristin! How wonderful to see you—and how splendid you look!"

A waft of familiar French perfume floated in the air as her mother brushed her cheek somewhere past Kristin's left ear. Anne Marie Nordwald was not fond of close physical contact.

Kristin stepped into the luxurious sitting room of the suite. "Hello, Mother. You're looking pretty splendid yourself. I like your outfit."

Anne Marie smiled with satisfaction, not attempting to downplay her daughter's compliments. "You like my robe? It's new."

She flung out her arms again and twirled in a succession of graceful circles toward the center of the room. The pale pink swansdown trimming of her negligee swirled around her as she moved. She looked, Kristin thought wryly, like a glamorous transplant from an old thirties movie. It only needed Fred Astaire to glide in from stage right and the scene would be perfect.

Instead, it was her father who entered the room, precisely on cue. He kissed his wife and beamed happily as he caught sight of his daughter, crushing her to him in a generous hug. Unlike his wife, Frederick Nordwald enjoyed the warmth of physical contact.

"Kristin, we are so glad you have come! It is most good to see you again."

Perhaps because he spent so much time in Europe working with musicians who spoke a multitude of different languages, her father retained slight traces of a foreign accent.

"Why are you in Vienna, little one?" he asked, his arm still around her shoulders. "Your cable did not tell us. Have you come to hear the new symphony by Vanderheym? It is a masterpiece, you know, and the concert will be a triumph. Vanderheym is certainly the most brilliant new composer we have seen since Schoenberg. Not that he is in the same style as Schoenberg, you understand; his music is traditionally melodic. But you will remember that I have never admired Schoenberg's insistence upon artificial form—"

Kristin burst out laughing, reaching up to touch her fingers lightly to her father's mouth. "Stop talking for a minute! Let me answer your questions before you give me a lecture on Schoenberg. No, Dad, I didn't come to Vienna to hear a new symphony. I came with Grey. He has business in Europe."

"Ah! Grey is here, too? That is very good. He is a splendid young man, and I am sure he will be most successful in his career. When we met, you know, I could see that he was extremely intelligent, even though he has no understanding of music. He has no ear, you know, none at all."

"And no singing voice, either," Anne Marie interjected sadly. "But he's a very handsome young man. He'd look wonderful in tights. I've often thought, Kristin, that he'd make the most marvelous Don Giovanni. His eyes are so dark, so expressive, he'd be perfect in the part. Except, of course, that he would have to sing. Such a pity." Her exquisite features took on an expression of lingering melancholy as she contemplated her son-in-law's lack of musical talent.

Kristin was amazed to find that she was genuinely amused. For the first time in her life, she found her parents' obsession with classical music endearing rather than infuriating.

"You know something? You two are impossible," she said lightly. "I can't believe that, until I met Grey, I never realized there are about a billion people in the world who are no more musical than I am."

This time it was her father's turn to smile. His hug tightened as he spoke. "Let us not exaggerate, little one. There are probably no more than half a billion people who are less musical than you. You are, you know, quite spectacularly unmusical."

"That must be why Grey and I make such a good

couple," she said cheerfully. "We can sing together in the shower and never know how disastrously out of tune we are. We sound terrific to us."

Anne Marie winced. "Two voices like yours, Kristin, singing in unison . . . I must say, my imagination boggles at the thought. Fortunately."

"Why don't we sit down?" her father suggested. "Where is Grey? He is working here in Vienna? He will be here for the concert tonight?"

"No." Kristin struggled to keep her voice entirely relaxed and natural. "He's attending a convention in Prague. They're discussing new energy sources for the eighties, or some such thing, and he's reading a paper about shale oil that he and his boss worked on together."

Anne Marie Nordwald sank onto a love seat, her pale pink ruffles floating out around her. "Prague is a beautiful city. Mozart directed the first performance of *Don Giovanni* at the National Theater there in 1787."

"Was it not 1786?" Frederick Nordwald asked.

Kristin sprang to her feet, placing herself squarely between her two parents. "I expect you're having a party after the concert tonight," she said firmly. "May I come?"

Her parents' attention was successfully returned to the present. "But, of course, you need not ask!" said her father. "We shall so much enjoy having you there. And we have already received a request from somebody who wants to meet you."

Frederick Nordwald crossed to a bureau set under the window and rustled through a small bundle of papers. "Ah, here it is. We received a cable from Narina Meriosova yesterday. We met her in San Francisco two years ago and liked her very much. She is a charming woman: It is tragic about her husband and her son."

"She loves her husband so much," Anne Marie said. "You can see it when she dances. She pours her heart out on the stage. Yet he doesn't seem to care for her."

"She told me herself that her husband doesn't permit their child to write to her," Frederick Nordwald said.

"All in all, it is a sad story. Anyway, Kristin, she says you two have friends in common, and she is anxious to meet you. She will be coming to our party tonight, so we will be able to introduce you to each other."

Kristin folded her hands tightly in her lap. Mr. Smith, she reflected, seemed to be arranging everything with great efficiency. She hoped his arrangements inside Czechoslovakia were proving equally efficient for Grey, Mikhail, and Grigori. She pushed the thought of Grey out of her mind. It was better, if she could possibly manage it, not to think about him.

She smiled at her parents. "I'd already heard Narina Meriosova would be in Vienna," she said. "I'll certainly be delighted to meet her."

She had lunch with her parents; then, in the afternoon, she went out to the Kärtnerstrasse and bought a dress to wear to the party. Succumbing to the romantic aura of the city, she chose a midnight-blue satin gown with a low neck and a full, draped skirt. The dress looked almost as if it had been designed for a ball at the Imperial Palace sometime around the turn of the century. There was no way in the world she was ever going to have an occasion to wear it once she returned to Denver, but she justified the outrageous number on the charge slip by telling herself it was important to appear to be caught up in the Viennese social whirl. She didn't want journalists or any other observers to think she looked worried.

Her parents' party started late that night in one of the Bristol's most ornate private dining rooms. The Viennese loved music, late nights, and parties in about equal proportion, and at midnight the celebration was barely beginning. Kristin remembered how, as a teenager, she had always felt drab and insignificant at her parents' parties. Tonight, when she would have been quite happy to appear inconspicuous, she was surprised to find herself attracting quite a lot of attention. She waited with mounting tension for Narina Meriosova's arrival, glad that her childhood experiences made it relatively easy for her to cope with the sort of sophisticated chatter needed at a party like this one.

She soon realized that William Vanderheym, the genius whose symphony had evoked such immense critical acclaim, entirely lacked her useful experience. He was a fair-skinned young American who blushed and stuttered every time a stranger spoke to him. Her mother and father were surrounded by their usual court of admirers and would-be interviewers, so Kristin eventually took pity on the young man, shielding him from pushy guests who wanted to converse with the music world's latest genius and helping him to sound coherent when a journalist requested an interview.

Mr. Vanderheym was embarrassingly grateful.

"Don't mention it," she said at last. "I never realized just how much I'd learned over the years about handling press interviews. I'm beginning to discover that there are some definite advantages to being brought up as the only daughter of two world-famous celebrities."

"Gee, I can't imagine what it would be like to grow up living in the same house as Frederick Nordwald and Anne Marie Nordwald. The conversations you must have had! The music... the lessons from both of them..." William Vanderheym's voice faded into a rapturous silence.

Kristin bit her lip to cut off a gurgle of laughter. There was something about being married, she thought, that was making her see her past in a completely new light. However, she suspected that Mr. Vanderheym was too young and much too earnest to appreciate the joke.

"My parents certainly live and breathe music," she said.

Her father arrived in front of them at that moment, a fragile, dark-haired woman leaning on his arm. What Grey had said was true, Kristin thought. Narina Meriosova curved herself against a man's body as naturally and instinctively as a flower directed its petals toward the sun.

"Kristin, here is Narina Meriosova," her father said. "She is looking forward to talking with you. But I am afraid I must deprive you of William's company. The director of the Salzburg Symphony wants to meet him."

Mr. Vanderheym blushed a shade somewhere between purple and fuchsia. He mumbled an almost incomprehensible good-bye to Kristin, then hurried away in the wake of her father.

Kristin held out her hand to Narina Meriosova. It was a strange sensation to meet the woman who had caused such an incredible upheaval in her once tranquil life.

"Mrs. Hamilton, it is a great pleasure to know you." Narina's accent was strong, although her grammar was perfectly correct.

"And I'm delighted to meet you. I've admired your work ever since I saw you dance in New York," Kristin responded truthfully. "I'm hoping to see you dance again before too long. When are you going to come to Denver?"

"I was there only a couple of weeks ago, Mrs. Hamilton. Perhaps you did not see the advertisements for my performance?"

"No, I guess I didn't. But Grey, my husband, may have mentioned that you were in town." Kristin cleared her throat, aware that her palms were becoming damp where they clutched her silver evening purse. Lord, but she wasn't very good at this sort of thing! Even now she couldn't quite believe that this guarded conversation was necessary. Who on earth was likely to be listening to them?

She cleared her throat again. "My mother tells me that you've never been to Vienna before, Miss Meriosova. I was here when I was a child, and I'm fairly familiar with most of the main attractions. I'd love to visit a few of them with you tomorrow, if you have time."

"I would like that. I would like that very much. And

if we are to spend time together, there is no reason for us to be so formal. Please call me Narina."

"Thank you. And, of course, you must call me Kristin." She reached into her purse, retrieved a tissue, and wiped her sticky hands. Good grief, she wondered, did this conversation sound as stilted as she feared it did?

"We could meet at noon, perhaps," Narina said. "I must dance tomorrow night, but we could pass two or three hours together."

"Yes, noon would be fine. I'll come to your room to pick you up. We'll have fun, I'm sure."

"Certainly." For an instant Narina Meriosova's eyes reflected a depth of anguish unlike anything Kristin had ever seen. Then she smiled. "The weather forecast is for more sunshine. Certainly we will have fun. That is what Vienna is all about, no?"

The next day they climbed all three hundred and forty-five stairs to the top of the south tower of St. Stephen's Cathedral. Kristin was puffing by the time they reached the top, though she prided herself on her physical fitness. Narina looked as fresh as if she had come up in the elevator and was raring to tackle another three hundred steps.

"Heavens, Narina, couldn't you gasp a little bit and make the rest of us feel better?" Kristin complained.

Narina laughed. "Come and visit with me after the performance tonight, if you wish to see me truly exhausted." She glanced back at the narrow staircase. "It's a good feeling to know those same stairs have been in use for almost eight hundred years. I like to feel—how do you say it?—continuity."

"I wonder what the people saw when they got to the top of this tower in the twelfth century," Kristin remarked.

"Forests, I expect. And maybe a few cultivated fields just around the cathedral." Narina leaned against the guardrail. "I love living in America, but I have learned to think with a different time frame when I am there. To most Americans a fifty-year-old building is antique. A hundred-year-old building is already an ancient monument."

Kristin grinned. "Maybe in New England that's true, or in the South. Denver's grown so fast that, in the area where we live, a ten-year-old house is considered a relic from the distant past."

Narina smiled as she pointed toward the southeast. "It is so clear today that you can see the Hungarian border. Over there, you see?"

Kristin glanced down at her guidebook. "It's only forty miles away. We could drive there in less than an hour if we wanted to."

"The Czech border is even closer." Narina hesitated for a fraction of a second, then she said, "Did you know that Austria has borders with seven different countries? If you live here, I think your view of world politics must be very different from the view of somebody living in the center of the United States."

Kristin looked hastily around. There was nobody within earshot. "The countries with Communist governments—Czechoslovakia and Hungary—is it easy to visit them from here? Is it . . . is it easy to cross the border?"

Narina turned her back on the spectacular view, her eyes meeting Kristin's with a fleeting gleam of sympathy. "If you have the right visas and travel documents, there is not much trouble. Hungary and Czechoslovakia encourage tourists. Like most other countries, they need the foreign currency that international tourists bring."

A group of schoolchildren clattered past, chattering noisily. "I think we should go to see the Hofburg now," Kristin said, knowing she shouldn't pursue the subject of boundary crossings. "Did you know that the Hofburg is the old Imperial Palace? We can walk there. It isn't too far."

At the Hofburg they saw the stables that housed the famous Lippizaner stallions before going into the main building and touring the private apartments once used by the Emperor Franz Josef and the Empress Elizabeth. As always when she visited a palace, Kristin came to the conclusion that Their Imperial Highnesses must have lived in a state of considerable physical discomfort. She wondered if ruling an empire compensated for the chill of the icy winter winds that must have rattled through the ornate, damask-draped bedchambers.

Narina spent a long time looking at the cradle that had once rocked the infant Napoleon, King of Rome, the son of Emperor Napoleon Bonaparte of France and his royal Austrian bride.

"It is very sad, I think," she said to Kristin. "Napoleon conquered half the world, but, in the end, he could not even obtain permission to see his own child. The baby who slept in that cradle was a virtual prisoner from the moment of his birth. He was called Emperor of the French, King of Rome, Duke of Reichstadt, yet his mother disliked him, his grandfather kept him imprisoned in a gloomy castle, and his father died not knowing if his son had even received his letters. The poor child's health was so badly neglected that he died when he was twenty. I have often thought that, when we give birth, we deliver a frighteningly powerful hostage into the hands of fortune."

Kristin was startled by the obvious parallels between Napoleon's story and Narina's own separation from her child. For the first time she understood exactly what Grey had been afraid of when he'd rejected her plea to become pregnant. Love of a child was a very potent weapon in the hands of an enemy, perhaps more potent than any other, because parents felt not only love but also responsibility for their children.

She touched Narina gently on the arm, urging her away from the empty cradle. The symbolism was too obvious to be bearable. "You haven't lost Grigori," she said quietly. "Don't give up hope, Narina. Not now."

"Even if Grigori returns to me tomorrow, I have lost

nearly four years of his life. A mother probably has only sixteen years when she can claim her son for her own; after that the world takes him over. If you think of it, Kristin, I have lost a quarter of my child's life."

Until that moment Narina and her family had been little more than abstract figures in Kristin's mind. Tragic figures, perhaps, but lacking emotional substance. Narina's words changed that forever. As they walked away from the infant Napoleon's cradle, Kristin was suddenly aware of pride, even a touch of relief, to know that Grey possessed the skills and the training that might enable Narina to be reunited with her husband and son.

It was late afternoon as they walked back to the hotel. Kristin waited until she was sure nobody was anywhere within earshot before she asked the question that had been burning on her tongue all day. "Do you know when they're going to leave?" she asked. "Do you think there will be an announcement on the television news saying that Mikhail and Grigori are missing from the conference?"

Narina's glance was almost pitying. "There will be no announcements," she said. "The authorities will hope to recapture them before any Western observers realize they are gone. Communist governments do not inform their citizens of anything unless it is in their own interest to do so."

The question was torn from Kristin before she could cut it off. "Oh, God, Narina, how are they going to make it across the border? How are they even going to make it out of Prague?"

"Thankfully, I have no idea. It is good to know that we cannot inadvertently betray them, is it not?"

Kristin smiled tightly. "I'm supposed to be offering you moral support. It seems to be happening the other way around."

"I speak quietly and smile a lot because, if I once started to cry, I'm afraid I might never stop. Believe me, I am glad to have you with me, Kristin. It helps to know that there is somebody who cares as much as I do what is going on right now at that convention in Prague."

The four days that marked the scheduled duration of the conference were the longest four days Kristin had ever spent. She understood little German, but she searched the local newspapers, hoping to find some mention of the conference—anything that would reassure her that Grey, Mikhail, and Grigori were still alive. She found only one passing reference to the conference, a small article in the business section of the daily paper. It told her nothing she wanted to know.

Partly because she felt it was her duty, but chiefly because she liked Narina more and more, she spent a great deal of time with the ballerina. She was almost overwhelmed with admiration for the woman's iron self-discipline.

In their excursions around the city and after Narina's nightly performances at the Opera House they met the usual assortment of journalists, none of whom seemed to make any connection between the conference in Prague and Narina's presence in Vienna. Nevertheless, despite her long experience of journalistic tactlessness, Kristin was astonished at the brutal questions members of the press were quite willing to ask Narina.

She usually managed to take even the most probing and unjustifiable inquiries pretty much in her stride. On the few occasions when she seemed in danger of breaking down, Kristin was able to cover for her. She began to feel satisfaction, even a slight thrill of personal pride, when she was able to protect Narina or throw too-inquisitive journalists completely off the scent.

She also spent quite a lot of time with her parents. She was touched when she realized that they were staying on in Vienna largely because she was still there, and she gradually began to accept the fact that they did love her and even admired her successful career as a physiotherapist. Their intentions as parents had probably always been good, but for two people as talented and as obsessed with music as they were, good intentions hadn't been quite enough. The demands of their careers had often taken precedence over her needs, but now that she was an adult, she accepted—albeit with a touch of regret—that a certain ruthlessness was probably an essential element in the development of genius. It was something of a relief, she reflected wryly, to know that her own children were not likely to suffer from the same benign parental neglect. All in all, she decided, she was quite glad she wasn't a genius.

On the fifth morning after Grey had gone, Kristin found a tiny announcement in the newspaper to the effect that the People's Conference on the Peaceful Development of New Energy Sources had been brought to a successful conclusion in Prague. She pored over the complex German sentences, trying to translate precisely what they said. As far as she could make out, there was no hint that any untoward incident had occurred during the conference. The scientists had exchanged information in a spirit of true brotherhood. Plans were already being made for a new conference next year. She put the paper down. So where was Grey? Where were Mikhail and Grigori?

Narina appeared at her door an hour before they had agreed to meet. She looked pale, her delicate features drawn to an almost feverish translucence. She walked into the room and sat down on the edge of the bed.

"Today I do not think I can smile," she said. "Perhaps we should not go out."

"Then what are we going to do?" Kristin asked with a calculated lack of sympathy. "Stare at each other across the bed?"

"I don't know." Narina pulled a tissue from the box on the nightstand and proceeded to shred it. "They should have been here by now, I know it. Something has happened to them. They have been—"

She didn't finish her sentence. She took another tissue

and began to shred it into the same pile as the other one.

Kristin swallowed over the hard knot of fear that had wedged itself deep in her throat. "Narina, for the first time since I met you, I think you're talking nonsense," she said. "I have a great idea. We'll ask my parents to come with us on a trip to Mayerling. They're got a rented car, so we can drive through the Vienna Woods. We'll be back in time for you to rest before your performance."

"Tonight is my last performance here. How can I stay on in Vienna when my performances are finished? In one week's time I must be back in America, in New York. How can I leave here when I have not seen Mikhail and Grigori?"

"Maybe we should only worry about one day at a time, Narina. Today let's go to Mayerling. Tonight I'll come to admire your dancing. Tomorrow ... well, we'll worry about tomorrow when we get there."

If the preceding four days had seemed long, this fifth day seemed interminable. Kristin began to understand why the playwright Pirandello had described hell as endless waiting. She was startled when her father drew her to one side and hugged her gently. "Something is worrying you, little one. What is it?"

"Nothing, Dad." She tried to smile. "Just missing Grey, I guess. Vienna's supposed to be a city for lovers, isn't it?"

"He will be here soon? The conference is finished, I think."

"I guess he'll be back any minute. He didn't ... he didn't give me an exact time for his return."

Her father was silent for a moment. "If you should need help, Kristin, remember that your mother and I are both right here in Vienna."

"I'll remember." She squeezed his hand gratefully. "How about taking me out to dinner tonight somewhere fancy? I think I need a dose of Viennese chocolate and whipped cream to keep me going."

"It's a deal."

*   *   *

Narina received a standing ovation at the conclusion of her final performance. Kristin was waiting for her when she emerged from her dressing room, but neither of them spoke during the journey back to the hotel. They parted in the elevator with a subdued good night.

When Kristin entered her room and found it empty, her heart plummeted. She acknowledged then what she had been hoping to find. The room looked doubly empty because she had been praying Grey might be waiting in it.

She was scarcely surprised when she heard a knock at the door half an hour later and opened it to find Narina standing in the corridor. The ballerina's eyes were huge, haunted. "May I come in?"

Kristin stepped aside. "Of course. I couldn't sleep either."

Narina walked into the bedroom and began to pace up and down. "Something must have gone wrong. They cannot have meant to take so long. Grey knows I am scheduled here only until tomorrow. Something has happened to them! We will not see them again."

"You're wrong, Narina. Grey is very highly trained, and everybody says your husband is a brilliant man. Just because there's a slight delay doesn't mean we ought to give up hope."

Kristin struggled to keep the panic from her voice. She knew it would do no good for them to feed each other's incipient hysteria. Already she could see the black pit of fear opening at her feet. What if Grey never came back? What if he disappeared into the mists of the Soviet criminal justice system, and she never found out what had happened to him? What if Narina had to spend the rest of her life without ever hugging her son again?

Kristin went into the bathroom and got two glasses. She filled them with kirsch and handed one to Narina. "Here, drink this. I bought the bottle to take home as a gift for my supervisor at the hospital, but I figure right now we need it more than she does."

"Maybe we could get drunk," Narina suggested.

Kristin grimaced. "We could try. But I have to warn you that I usually throw up before I even begin to get merry."

Narina's laugh broke into a sob. "We are both too virtuous for our own good, no?"

Once Narina had started to cry, she couldn't stop. The tears flowed down her cheeks in an endless, choking stream. Kristin gathered the ballerina's slender body into her arms, feeling tears gather in her own eyes as she tried to find something comforting to say. She could think of nothing. If Grey didn't come back— She quickly slammed the door on that thought. She couldn't handle it at the moment.

"I have not cried in three and a half years." Narina's words were muffled by her weeping. "For three and a half years I would not let myself hope. I lived only to go out on the stage, where I could dance and sometimes forget about Grigori and Mikhail for two or three hours. Then, last month, your husband came to me and told me that Mikhail and Grigori would be in Prague, that they would be trying to cross the border into Austria."

Her crying finally stopped, and she walked over to the side of the bed to pull out another tissue. "I should not have allowed myself to hope. It is very painful to hope. I learned that many years ago. But sometimes we are foolish and forget our lessons, even when they have been learned the hard way."

"You're giving up too easily," Kristin said. "I obviously have more faith in Grey's ability than you do. He's going to come back, and he'll bring your husband and son with him, you'll see."

Narina blew her nose, then managed a smile. "American optimism! It is another reason why I like living in the States so much."

Kristin sat down on the bed, propping herself up against the pillows before reaching for her glass of kirsch. She took a large swallow. "I'll tell you what, Narina. This is tasting better and better."

Narina took a sip, then wrinkled her nose. "It's too sweet for me."

"We can't all grow up tossing back Russian firewater, you know." Kristin patted the bed. "We have a long night to fill. Come and sit next to me. Tell me how you first became a dancer."

"Well, my mother was a dancer and I grew up in a suburb of Moscow called—"

There was a loud knock on the door. Both women jumped up, kirsch slopping over their fingers as they rammed their glasses onto the bedside tables. Kristin, who happened to be on the left side of the bed, reached the door first.

Her fingers were trembling so badly she could hardly slip the catch on the lock. She finally succeeded, wrenching the door open with a violent tug.

Grey stood in the corridor, his face wreathed in smiles. He was filthy dirty, unshaven, and his eyes were bloodshot. To Kristin he had never looked more beautiful. Close beside him stood a tall, gaunt man and a scrawny little boy. The child had straw in his hair.

There was a shriek from behind her, then a rush of cool air as Narina launched herself into her husband's arms.

Mikhail didn't speak, nor did he make a sound. He didn't have to. His eyes had already said it all.

Chapter Twelve

KRISTIN GAVE A murmur of joy as Grey entered the bedroom and took her into his arms. He hugged her tight, smothering her with kisses. She ran her hands feverishly over his body, as if she wanted to assure herself that he was really and truly there. It was a long time before she had breath to speak.

"You smell overwhelming," she said, laughing and crying at the same time. "A mixture of garlic and pigsty, I think."

"You have a discriminating nose, my dear. That's exactly what it is." He grinned, the familiar, lighthearted grin that she loved so much. "Don't you approve?"

She hugged him again. "On second thought, it smells wonderful!" She drew his head down for another kiss, realizing as she finally relaxed in his arms just how unbearably tense she had been for the last few days.

She was still clinging to Grey when Narina walked over to shake his hand. "Thank you," she said, reaching up to kiss his cheek. "What can I say? There's no possible way to show you my gratitude, no way I can ever repay my debt to you."

Grey touched his finger to her cheek. "Sure there is," he said softly. "Bring Grigori to see me when he's captain of his Little League team."

An emotional silence filled the bedroom; then with sudden briskness Grey extricated himself from Kristin's arms and walked over to the telephone. "I have to let people know we've arrived safely," he said. "We must get the Meriosovas to a U.S. army base as soon as we can. We don't want to embarrass the Austrian government if we can avoid it. They try to maintain good relations with their neighbors, so it's better if we hustle Mikhail and Grigori away as soon as possible."

Mikhail spoke to Kristin in halting English while Grey made his phone call. "I haf so many things to thank you and your husband for, I find no words in English. Perhaps not even in Russian."

"I saw your face, and Narina's, when you walked in the door. I don't need any other thanks."

Grigori, who had been standing to one side observing the proceedings with a certain detachment, suddenly burst into a stream of rapid Russian. Narina grabbed him by the wrist and rushed him into the bathroom. When they emerged five minutes later, she looked a little rueful. Grigori, his face and hands now spotlessly clean and his hair combed, looked wary and very pale.

"He was sick," Narina explained. "I suppose it is not surprising considering the way he says he traveled into Austria."

Grey got off the phone at that moment, and Kristin looked at him inquiringly. "We came in a farm truck carrying a load of piglets," he said. "But we only had papers for two adult men, so Grigori was concealed in a special compartment at the back of the truck."

"Oh lord, poor kid!" Kristin smiled at Grigori, but he refused to return her smile. On the whole, she thought, he didn't seem entirely thrilled to be here. She noticed that, although he clung tightly to his father's hand, his body remained stiff and unyielding where his mother held him. Narina had undoubtedly noticed his reluctance to touch her.

Kristin had a sudden inspiration. She went to the closet and retrieved her purse, searching in it until she found the pack of bubble gum she always carried to smooth over tense moments with her most difficult young patients. She came back to Grigori, talking to him even though she knew he couldn't understand her actual words.

"Look what I've found!" she said lightly. "This is cherry bubble gum, and this brand's a favorite with all the kids I know in America because they say it blows the biggest bubbles and it doesn't stick to your nose when it pops." She stripped off the outer packaging and unwrapped one of the pieces, sniffing appreciatively. "Mmm . . . smells real good!"

She popped it into her mouth, watching as Grigori's eyes followed her movements in silent fascination. She chewed vigorously for a little while, then stuck her tongue into the gum and blew with all the expertise she could muster. A huge, pale-pink bubble emerged from her lips. After a moment she popped it and pushed the gum back into her mouth. Grigori's expression slowly turned from hostility to guarded awe.

Kristin held out the package of gum. "Would you like it?" she asked casually. "I bet you could blow a giant bubble if you tried."

Grigori turned to look at his father, and Mikhail nodded, a slight smile alleviating the gauntness of his face. Grigori took the gum, saying something that was obviously intended to express his thanks for the gift. He immediately unwrapped a piece and put it in his mouth, chewing with total and ecstatic concentration.

Narina laughed, only a tiny catch of sadness in her

voice. "A half-forgotten mother is hard to accept. Bubble gum, apparently, is easier."

Mikhail tightened his arm around his wife's waist. "We have forever to let him know you. Now there is no hurry."

A quiet tap at the door heralded the arrival of four military people, tactfully clothed in civilian dress. When they had shown their identification to Grey, the senior officer spoke politely. "We've arranged transportation to the base for the Meriosovas, sir. We also have all the necessary documentation." He turned to Narina. "If you'll give us your room key, Mrs. Meriosova, one of my men will pack up all your belongings. I expect you'd like to have them with you at the base."

She handed over her key. "It's thoughtful of you, Major, but in comparison to having my husband and son, a few suitcases don't seem all that important."

"I imagine not. This must be a wonderful moment for you." The major turned once more to Grey. "We'll be leaving you to catch up on your rest then, sir. Congratulations on the success of your mission."

"Thanks." Grey yawned. "I feel like I have a lot of rest to catch up on."

Just as they were leaving the room, Narina turned back to hug Kristin. "Thank you for everything. Without you, I do not think I would have survived the last few days. When we are all back in the States, we will still be friends, no?"

"Yes, we certainly will."

The major closed the bedroom door, and Grey and Kristin were alone. The sound of footsteps faded quickly into silence.

Grey turned to her and smiled. "What a tactful group of soldiers! Did you notice that they never once mentioned the delicate odor of pig that's beginning to fill our bedroom?"

"They were impressed at being in the presence of so many heroes," she said, not teasing.

Grey actually blushed. "Aw, shucks, honey, it wasn't hardly nothing."

"How did they get here so fast, anyway?"

"They were on standby at the American Embassy. It's right on the Kärtnerstrasse, only a few minutes from here. Everything's been arranged to transport the Meriosovas to a base in West Germany. They're going by ambulance, so they'll be able to sleep."

"I expect you want to sleep as well."

"Eventually. Right now, more than anything, I want a shower. Somehow I don't think essence of piglet is ever going to catch on as perfume of the month."

"Well, now that you've mentioned it, I tend to agree. The tub, complete with oil of verbena bath essence and English lavender soap, is at your immediate disposal."

"Do you have a plastic bag where I can dump my clothes? From the way I've started to itch, I think they're probably full of an interesting assortment of insect life."

She gulped. "Fleas?"

He grinned. "Undoubtedly. Not to mention several other less attractive parasites."

She reached into the closet and handed him a plastic laundry bag. "Please tie it *tightly*, Grey."

It was a full thirty minutes before he came out of the bathroom, looking scrubbed and pink and considerably less exhausted. Kristin was lying in bed, the sheet pulled up around her shoulders. Grey crossed over to the bed and pushed the sheet down, smiling approvingly when he saw her nakedness.

"Well now, that's a welcome sight for weary eyes," he said as he sank onto the bed. He stretched luxuriously. "Only five days away, and I'd already forgotten how wonderful a regular mattress could feel!"

He closed his eyes, his hand resting idly but possessively on Kristin's breast. His breathing deepened.

"You can't go to sleep!" she exclaimed. "Grey, I've been alternately dying of curiosity and fright ever since you left. You have to tell me how you got out of Prague."

"I dressed up as a security guard and marched Mikhail and Grigori into a waiting limousine." He chuckled. "The other security guards saluted as we drove out of the convention center."

A ripple of fear raised goose bumps on her skin. Even though Grey was now safely back, she couldn't ignore how much danger he'd been in. She wondered what the penalties were in Czechoslovakia for impersonating a police officer. Probably twenty years in the salt mines at a minimum. She pressed her body close to his, instinctively seeking the warmth and security of his presence. She needed reassurance that the danger was truly past.

"Mmm . . . that feels good," Grey murmured sleepily. "Do it again."

She stroked her hands lightly all over his body. "How did you transform yourself from security chief to farmer?" she asked.

"Honey, it's a long story, but obviously we needed to have documentation to get across the border, and forgeries would have been too risky. We had somebody working in the Czech Ministry of Agriculture who was able to produce an export license and exit visas for us. That's all there was to it."

"Somehow I can't believe it was as easy as you're making it sound. You were later getting back than you planned to be, I'm sure of it."

He yawned. "I'm too tired to talk anymore, Kris. We did run into a spot of trouble when we went to pick up the truck and the livestock. We were supposed to meet one of my people in a wood near the border, but when we got there we found the place was already staked out. However, we made the rendezvous eventually, and nobody was hurt."

She shivered. "I think there's a big chunk of the story you just left out, Grey."

He opened his eyes, and she saw that they were full

of laughter. "You'll have to persuade me ever so skill-
fully if you want to hear the details," he said.

"I thought you were too tired to talk."

"I am. But I'm not planning to talk right now, so
there's no problem. I think it's probably going to take
you weeks of skillful seduction to get the story out of
me."

She sat up, putting her hands on her hips in mock
indignation. "Are you telling me you're planning to lie
there like a statue night after night while I make love to
you?"

"Sounds like an absolutely wonderful idea," he said.
"How about if I resist and you keep trying to persuade
me?"

She pummeled him with a pillow, and Grey retreated
down the bed, laughing. "Hey, how can you attack me
like this when you know I'm too weak to defend myself?"

She was immediately contrite, curling against him and
pressing soft kisses against his chest. "I'm sorry," she
said. "It's so wonderful to have you back that I keep
forgetting how exhausted you must be."

"Mmm...Funny, some of my energy seems to be
returning." He twisted suddenly, capturing her hands and
holding them back against the pillow. He lowered his
mouth to her throat, kissing the pulse that throbbed wildly
in the tiny hollow at its base.

"I've just remembered I made you a promise," he
said. "And you know I'm the sort of guy who never goes
back on his word."

Her mind was already beginning to spin off onto some
distant cloud of pleasure. "Promise?" she muttered
vaguely.

"We're going to make a baby, remember? As I recall,
you're going to lock me in a darkened room until I do
my duty and get you pregnant." He sighed. "Sounds like
a harsh punishment for a man who's just returned from
a perilous, death-defying mission."

A burning excitement, part pure sexual pleasure and

part joy, flooded her. "I'll try to make it easy for you," she breathed.

"Keep moving like that, and my imprisonment may not last out the night," he said with a groan. His mouth moved slowly down her body.

She gasped. "Oh, Grey, don't do that. Grey, please..." She gulped. "Please, don't stop!"

She felt his quiver of laughter before he reached up to claim her mouth in a crushing kiss. "That's what I really admire," he said. "A woman who knows her own mind."

"I know my own mind," she said softly. "I love you, Grey, and I know you love me. You told me once that that was the ultimate truth about our relationship, and you were right."

He kissed her long and deep, and her body arched up triumphantly to meet his. "I have the feeling we're creating a spectacular baby," he whispered.

"I hope not. I think I'd enjoy a few more weeks of trying."

He tightened his arms around her, and she responded with delight as he murmured words of love against her mouth. She had learned a great deal about Grey over the past couple of weeks, and she had learned even more about herself. Now they had the rest of their lives to complete the discoveries. It was a wonderful feeling.